# THUNDER

425-51

# THUNDER

**Adapted**
**By**

**Jean de Lascoumettes**

**Based on an original screenplay**
**By**

**Byron Morgan**

English Translation
By
**Eric McNaughton**

Philip J. Riley's

**LOST FILM SERIES**

BearManor Media
P.O. Box 1129
Duncan, OK 73534-1129

Phone: 580-252-3547
Fax: 814-690-1559

www.bearmanormedia.com

First U.S. printing by BearManor Media, 2014
Published in France, 1930 by Ferenczi & Sons
Based on the *Thunder* screenplay by Byron Morgan
Adapted to French by Jean de Lascoumettes, 1930
English Translation by Eric McNaughton, 2014



Special thanks to Dustin Jablonski, who provided a copy
of the original French novelette

ciné-volume
3 FRS 50
JEAN DE LASCOUMETTES
TONNERRE
ROMAN D'APRES LE FILM
INTERPRETE PAR
LON CHANEY
J. FERENCZI & FILS, EDITEURS
9 RUE ANTOINE CHANTIN PARIS
EDITION METRO-GOLDWYN-MAYER

LON
CHANEY
IN
THUNDER
WITH
PHYLLIS HAVER and
JAMES MURRAY
A
WILLIAM NIGH
PRODUCTION
A Metro · Goldwyn · Mayer Picture

# Thunder

Metro-Goldwyn-Mayer - 9 reels. 7,872 feet. *Released:* July 8, 1929. *Production halted:* April 30, 1929. *Resumed:* May 13 to May 23, 1929. *Retakes:* May 28,1929 and June 1, 1929, 56 days. Released with sound effects and musical score (Movietone). *Producer:* Hunt Stromberg. *Director:* William Nigh. *Scenario:* Byron Morgan and Ann Price, from a story by Byron Morgan. *Titles:* Joseph Farnham. *Photographer:* Henry Sharp. *Film Editor:* Ben Lewis. *Script Supervisor:* Willard Sheldon. *Assistant Director: Frank Messenger. Unit Production Manager:* Jerry Mayer. *Still Photographer:* Bert Lynch. *Production costs:* $352,000. *Box Office Gross $624.000*

*Courtesy of the MGM Legal Department*

## Cast

Lon Chaney - Grumpy Anderson
Phyllis Haver - Zella
James Murray- Tommy
Tom Keene- Jim
Frances Norris - Molly
Wally Albright, Jr. - Davey
John MacIntosh - Railroad Man

1929 - "Chaney was suffering a great deal, not only from his back and the general fatigue, but his throat was painful and irritated as well. Like the trouper he was, Chaney ignored his illness and went ahead with plans for his newest silent feature—*Thunder*. The film centered around an old railroad engineer by the name of "Grumpy" Anderson, who is nearing the end of his career and having a difficult time adjusting to it. There is a subplot involving his son, who worked with him on the railroad and a movie actress traveling by train. The film opens with a terrible blizzard which necessitated moving production out of California, Green Bay, Wisconsin was one of the sites chosen and Chaney headed East along with Jeske (Chaney's assistant and right-hand man) to assist him. The making of *Thunder* would be fraught with complications after complication with everything from the equipment and weather to the actors themselves. Co-star James Murray had a serious problem with alcohol and required someone constantly nearby to monitor his level of intoxication. Chaney, much to his chagrin and contrary to everything he stood for, held up production for a time due to illness. His weakened physical condition made him vulnerable to a virus which laid him low for days at a time. Chaney stubbornly pushed with filming and caused the virus to progress into full blown "walking" pneumonia. Even though Chaney was able to perform adequately in the part, he did require the use of a double for some of the more physically challenging shots, as well as a double to actually operate the locomotive (due to strict railroad regulations). Jeske provided the perfect choice for a double, as he had doubled for Chaney in the past, and was made up roughly to simulate Chaney's appearance. Jeske would only be seen from the back, or maybe a quick side shot, so full make-up wasn't necessary. He already had a moustache which could be easily touched up with grey to match Chaney's "old man" make up for Grumpy. (Which Chaney had based on his real life father Frank)

When asked about Chaney, Norma Shearer (actress and wife of MGM boss Irving Thalberg) said, "Lon Chaney relied heavily on his man [Jeske], more so in the last years when he was weakened by his illness. That was his assistant in *Thunder* doing the jumps. They looked very much alike.

*Thunder* would finally reach the theatres on July 8, 1929. By this time Chaney's health had deteriorated to the point where the studio heads at MGM were becoming extremely nervous. It was rumored that a piece of artificial snow used in the filming parts of *Thunder* lodged in Chaney's throat and caused further inflammation and allowed an infection to set in. Chaney struggled with his malady as best he could, but he could not deny the fact he was no longer able to work. Chaney had to bow out of a picture he'd been slated to star in *(The Bugle Sounds)* and was suspended by MGM from his lucrative new contract on July 25th, 1929, until he was able to work again."

[From "Lon Chaney's Shadow - John Jeske and the Chaney Mystique" by Suzanne Gargiulo.]

"Audiences stood and cheered for Chaney in the exciting climax of *Thunder."* Chauncey Haines, Silent Film Organist - Performed at the Los Angeles premiere - in 1929.

THUNDER was Lon Chaney's last silent film. When he recuperated enough he finally went back to MGM in April of 1930 to complete his only talking picture, *The Unholy Three.* A few months after its release he was hospitalized again. He died August 26th 1930.

# NORTH WESTERN LINES

Official Publication of the
Chicago & North Western Historical Society

Vol. 10, No. 3
Summer 1983
$3.50

In this view, "Pop" and Chaney line-up a few details for the next scene. Film makers rely heavily on the expertise of railroaders such as Mr. Pruner to quickly grasp their needs and enable them to get their "takes" in the shortest possible time. Photo from the collection of Philip B. Korst.

# "Thunder" on the C&NW

By Philip B. Korst

By 1929 actor Lon Chaney was a top Hollywood star, and is perhaps remembered most for his role as the *Hunchback Of Notre Dame* in an early film version of that epic. The nation's railroads were frequently the setting or subject for films in the early part of the century. The movies came to the C&NW when, in early 1929, MGM made the film *Thunder* which starred Mr. Chaney on the then Lake Shore Division. Mr. Lindsay E. Pruner, the C&NW trainmaster at Green Bay, was given the very interesting assignment of working with the movie's cast and film crews. We thank Philip B. Korst, a grandson of Mr. Pruner and also a retiree of the C&NW, for this interesting story on the making of the film and the friendship which his grand-dad formed with Mr. Chaney.

*Editor*

**EARLY 1929 WAS AN EXCITING TIME** for the North Western's Lake Shore Division. Metro-Goldwin-Mayer was to be on location in the Green Bay area to film the movie *Thunder*. Lon Chaney would star in his first "talkie" as the locomotive engineer, Bill Nye would be his fireman, and Phyllis Haver would provide the love interest.

My grandad, Lindsay E. Pruner, trainmaster at Green Bay, was assigned as the liaison between the C&NW and M-G-M. His first job was to teach Lon how to actually operate a locomotive. My grandad liked to tell what an apt pupil Lon was. One day when Lon was "soloing," Pruner stood outside the depot at Little Chute and held up an order hoop. This had not been part of the instruction, but Lon was equal to the occasion and reached out of the cab window, scooping up the order hoop in true railroader style.

Chaney passed his exam and was qualified as a North Western hogger on March 29, 1929. Pruner, who had retained his Brotherhood of Locomotive Engineers membership, tried to get the Brotherhood to make Lon an honorary member, but was turned down by Grand Chief Johnston in Cleveland. Now days everyone recognizes the benefits of good public relations.

**MY GRANDAD AND LON DEVELOPED** a fond relationship. Lon called him "Pop," and, of course, "Pop" was

14 Summer 1983 NORTH WESTERN LINES

Part of the crew are shown here with the movie train pulled by engine 2578, a class J. Mikado type. From left to right are: Bill Nye, fireman, Phillis Haver, Mr. Pruner, Lon Chaney, two unidentified M-G-M crew members, two C&NW officials, the second of which is probably Jack Rice, Superintendent and Jerry Mayer of M-G-M. On the pilot deck are two unidentified workmen. Photo from the collection of Philip B. Korst.

fascinated by the mysteries of movie-making. He used to tell me of how they filmed a man doing a little dance, then slipping and falling off the top of a box car one day, filming a switch engine supposedly running over him on the next day, and on the third day they shot the scene where his lifeless body was picked up off the track.

Wisconsin's March weather can be severe, and shortly after his return to Hollywood, Chaney was hospitalized. Pruner sent him the following telegram:

> Dear Lon:
>
> News of your illness received with deepest regrets. I am boosting for you. Don't let her slip and you will make the grade. My best wishes for a speedy recovery.

Lon Chaney replied with this wire:

> Dear Pop:
>
> Your wire received and bless your old heart. I want to thank you for your kind consideration. Am not dangerously ill just had a touch of pneumonia and pleurisy but everything is lovely now. Will be out of bed in three or four days. Tell the bunch hello and keep my kindest thoughts for yourself. Yours for better engineers and weather.
>
> Lon Chaney

Pop retired and visited Southern California in 1933, but by then Lon Chaney had passed on to that great main line where all the lights are green.

**SEVERAL YEARS AGO I WAS BROWSING** in a book store and found a book entitled, *Life On A Locomotive*, by George Williams (Howell-North Books, 1050 Parker Street, Berkley, Ca 94710). The book was about his father, Buddy Williams, and his experiences as a fireman and hogger on the C&NW, so I bought it immediately. It was not until I reached chapter eight in the book that I discovered the chapter was all about L. E. Pruner. My grandad had been Buddy William's favorite engineer when Williams was firing.

Later I was able to entertain George Williams in my home. He had written his dad in California, and Buddy, then 88, had written the following in response:

> I never enjoyed a man more than Len. We made money 16 hours a day and enjoyed every minute of it. The Sup and all the big shots would call him in for advice.

Behind the locomotive was a camera car with the usual lights, cables and the countless people necessary to shoot a movie. To the extreme left is Lon Chaney, who certainly looks like a hogger. This photo was made in March of 1929, much to the surprise of the Hollywood crew, they had snow to contend with. Photo from the collection of Philip B. Korst.

We had an enjoyable visit. Of course George and I and our wives had fun reminiscing about life on the railroad before diesels, CTC, or the twelve hours of service law.

About a year after *Thunder* was filmed, the movie *Danger Lights* was made on the Milwaukee Road, which I understand is still available today. To the best of my knowledge, however, *Thunder* is no longer in print.

*[Ed. Note: The film* Danger Lights *is still shown by Public Broadcasting Channels on TV occasionally, so watch your program listings. If anyone has further information on the film,* Thunder, *we would appreciate their sharing it with us.]*

STÅL MOT STÅL
LON CHANEY
PHYLLIS HAVER
JAMES MURRAY
REGI:
WILLIAM NIGH
Metro-Goldwyn-Mayer
"EN ALLDELES ÖVERDÅDIG, SPÄNNANDE
OCH DRAMATISK FILM" VÅRA NÖJEN
ENSAMRÄTT: FILM-A:B. LE MAT-METRO-GOLDWYN, STOCKHOLM

LON
CHANEY
IN
Thunder
with PHYLLIS HAVER
JAMES MURRAY
A
WILLIAM NIGH
PRODUCTION
Story by Byron Morgan...
Continuity by Byron Morgan
and Ann Price-Titles by
Joe Farnham-Directed by
WILLIAM NIGH
A Metro-Goldwyn-Mayer
PICTURE

# Chapter I

Winter, in the Rocky Mountains. The great white silence is torn with a thunderclap. This is the snow storm. The horizon is lost in a cold gray, white in the valleys; white on the peaks and slopes. And the sky is full of dancing snowflakes which seem to burst.

The short route runs through the vast tumultuous desert, barely visible, it is like a black wound in the snow which covers everything. It climbs up the hills and down the mountainside. It flees dizzily from this terrifying desolation.

And the engine, buffeted by the storm, heaving, digging its way with great pushes of its snowplow, like a distracted beast trying to clear a path.

In the engine, old Grumpy Anderson, its soul. And Tommy Anderson, his son, the driver.

Grumpy Anderson has been a railway engineer for more than 20 years. For a long time he has led the fast trains, taking responsibility like all men of science, will and heart.

For more than 20 years, Grumpy Anderson has been a slave to time, to the hour, the minute and the second. Respect of time has become, for him, a new religion. His duty is to this time, this precise and strict time. He would feel like a dishonest man if he didn't adhere strictly to the Company's timetable.

Also, how he loves his engine! He loves it not as a thing, but as a living being. He loves it because it is powerful, flexible and docile, because it obeys his desire and never refuses any new effort he asks of it. When he adjusts its speed, its vagaries of flight, handles the regulators, the controls, the brake, it seems that it speaks by signs, a trusted friend, immensely powerful and always submissive.

He spends many hours on it, watching it, tending it, bringing it to life! They are together, bound by strong emotions, they have experienced similar hardships. What would he be without it? If it had not gracefully consented to be his? And he wondered conceitedly: "What would it be without me?"

But there are things against which the will alone can not prevail.

Grumpy Anderson, in the midst of the storm that struck and envelopes them, watches the dials and gauges. All is well. Pressure is maintained. Everything works perfectly. And yet there is no progress. The constant fight against snow wears down and wastes the forces of the iron monster. They lose seconds every kilometer. When will they arrive?

There would obviously have to be an apology. It is an apology well used for foggy days or snowfall, that trains suffer delays. Of course. But Grumpy Anderson has never known this shame. He is strong enough to laugh at everything.

Feverishly he look at his watch. The seconds are running too fast.

"Keep the pressure up, Tommy!"

Tommy is a handsome fellow, a son who works alongside his father. Tirelessly he shovels coal into the mouth of the incandescent engine: "Eat! Eat! Feed yourself!"

With a large shovel, sweating despite the cold, he shovels the black food. But he has no sooner started shovelling when his father's voice yells through the storm.

"Coal! Coal!".

Tommy looks at the control panel. The gauge needle is fixed to the red line that indicates danger. They continue to fill the boiler so it is impossible to let go as the engine blindly goes at will towards the narrowing horizon.

"Tommy, look! The way is clear?"

Eyebrows furrowed under the blows of the clawing wind, heat stinging his eyes.

"Clear, father!"

Clear! With a shot, the engine is projected along the rails. Grumpy Anderson precipitates the arrival of steam in the chambers. Faster! Always faster! Despite the snow, despite the sky, despite everything, the train must arrive on time. ...

"Look, Tommy! The way is clear?....Coal, Tommy!... The way, Tommy!...."

The older Anderson is still sure of his hands, his nerves, his courage. He no longer has complete faith in his eyes, completely burned by incandescent glow of the fire, dried by the wind, bruised by the rain. Ah! If he were twenty years old! But is his son not there to assist him, to replace him,to learn this trade, his life's trade, this job which is all his life?

"Clear?"

And Tommy signals, nods his head.

He knows very well, too, that they will be asked to account why earlier they had already been delayed at the station, and people get impatient or worry and now they look at the engineer and driver with dark reproachful eyes .... But , is it convenient to arrive at the second stated on the draconian schedule at all costs? He does not think so, this superstition about the time, this exaggerated respect for the time. If old Grumpy wasn't there, the engine would blow a little, and hurried travelers would be a reason. But his father is there.

And it is really very well that this old man is a slave bounden by duty, a relentless order. He's a handsome old man whose heart beats for pistons, whose cold resolution and iron will appear to animate this beast of metal.

"The way is clear?"

The signal is passed, away, burned, useless.

"The way is clear, father!"

# CHAPTER II

28 minutes late! 28 minutes and a few hundred kilometers from their goal! Will they be on time?

No. Under the relentless urging of Grumpy, the train leaped ahead and rushed forward. Masses of snow build up at the bow of the engine, dense and compact. As the engine flies in the face of the wind, it is buffeted, the force of the win rebounding on the walls of metal.

Nevertheless. Shaking with, impatience, the locomotive advances. The dizzying kilometers race by.

Grumpy Anderson looks at his watch. OK. They are making up time. Bit by bit they are making up the precious time they lost. . More than 28 minutes. Now, it's not more than 22 minutes. Now down to 15. Soon it will be only 9.

9 minutes! Everything is going to be fine! Nothing can prevent them now from arriving on time! Not much left to make up.

"Father!"

"What's up?"

"A red light! The way isn't clear!"

Grumpy reverses the steam. Tommy throws on the

brakes. In the uproar of wheels jumping the switches, the train stops at a burnt out station.

The engine, full of steam, pants and then stops. Grumpy jumps on the ballast.

"They're going to make us lose 5 minutes! .... This is just our luck…."

But Tommy just mocks the situation! Why should they be concerned about matters which are not their problem? Is it their fault if they are prevented from continuing their journey? They will arrive soon enough.

And he gets down to stretch his legs, to feel the hard ground on which it is so good to walk, and which does not have mood swings of the deck of a locomotive.

Certainly, it is not only that the train is being driven by his father that the trouble occurs. There are - and this is why they have stopped – the other trains halted ahead.

The passengers take the worst philosophically view of the world for the most part.

A phonograph in the saloon car of Anderson's train, played a foxtrot, and couples danced to pass the time, improvising their steps. What did the weather matter? They had warm sheltered windows on which the frost made strange patterns. And for the rest, they will still arrive soon enough .... it's not pressing.

Tommy, who hadn't anything else to do, while his father checked, like a watchmaker checking his watch, the huge wheels of engine, attracted by the music, went through to the car where the couples were whirling.

A handsome boy, Tommy Anderson!

With clear, bright, laughing eyes. He was well built and sturdy, enjoying life. He had red lips and no fog or winds had tanned his face and he was not able to be shy, or even blush

Youth in all its adorable innocence. The rigid principles in which he was raised, the hard work he was obliged to do under the his father's direction, had kept him from the ordinary pleasures of young men of his age.

He knew little of life. He knew nothing of its hypocrisies or conventions. Life seemed nice because he was healthy and had an uncomplicated soul.

Women seemed to him desirable, for the same reason, and he had not yet had an experience that killed that spontaneity or made him reflect on being the most thoughtless.

As Tommy was going along the car full of cheerful people, a pretty girl, who was dancing alot, made circles by pressing her lips on the glass. An amusing child? Or pretend kisses without purpose or direction? Her lips were tantalizing, her gaze hypnotic. Furthermore, her loneliness also created, who knows what mystery in her penetrating look, her wink of the eye, in her destiny.

To tell the truth, Tommy did not think too much about it. He wasn't embarrassed by the subtleties.

Like a little boy, he knocked on the window and gave a big smile.

Surprisingly, the unknown girl doesn't seem offended at all. Cheekily, she sticks out her tongue.

"You are very pretty" says Tommy frankly.

She couldn't hear his words through the glass wall. Nevertheless, because that movement of his lips or the look in his eyes ,she understood,and she replied with a wink.

*The regulations forbid it, Miss. That's enough reason.*

*Ah well grandfather. . .we're here anyway.*

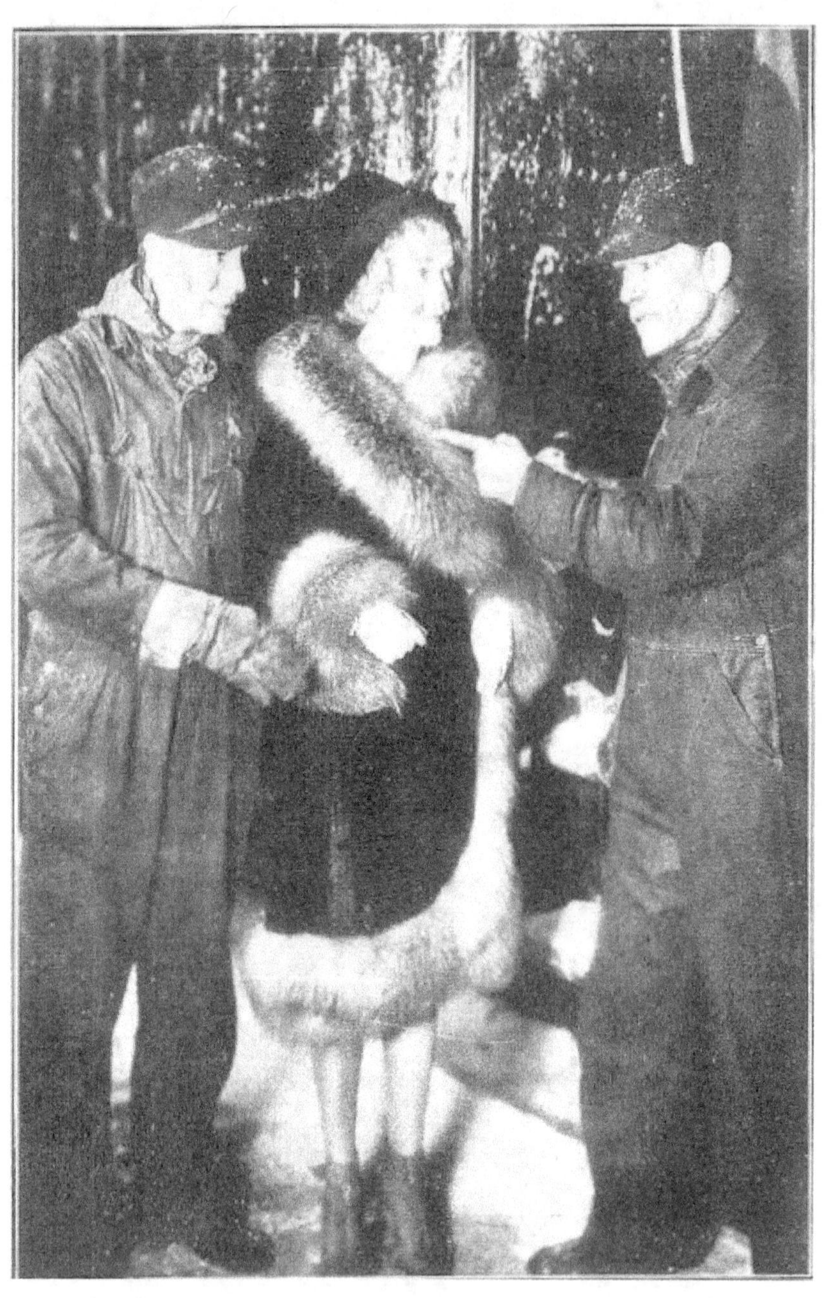

*You. Shut up. And hide. . .*

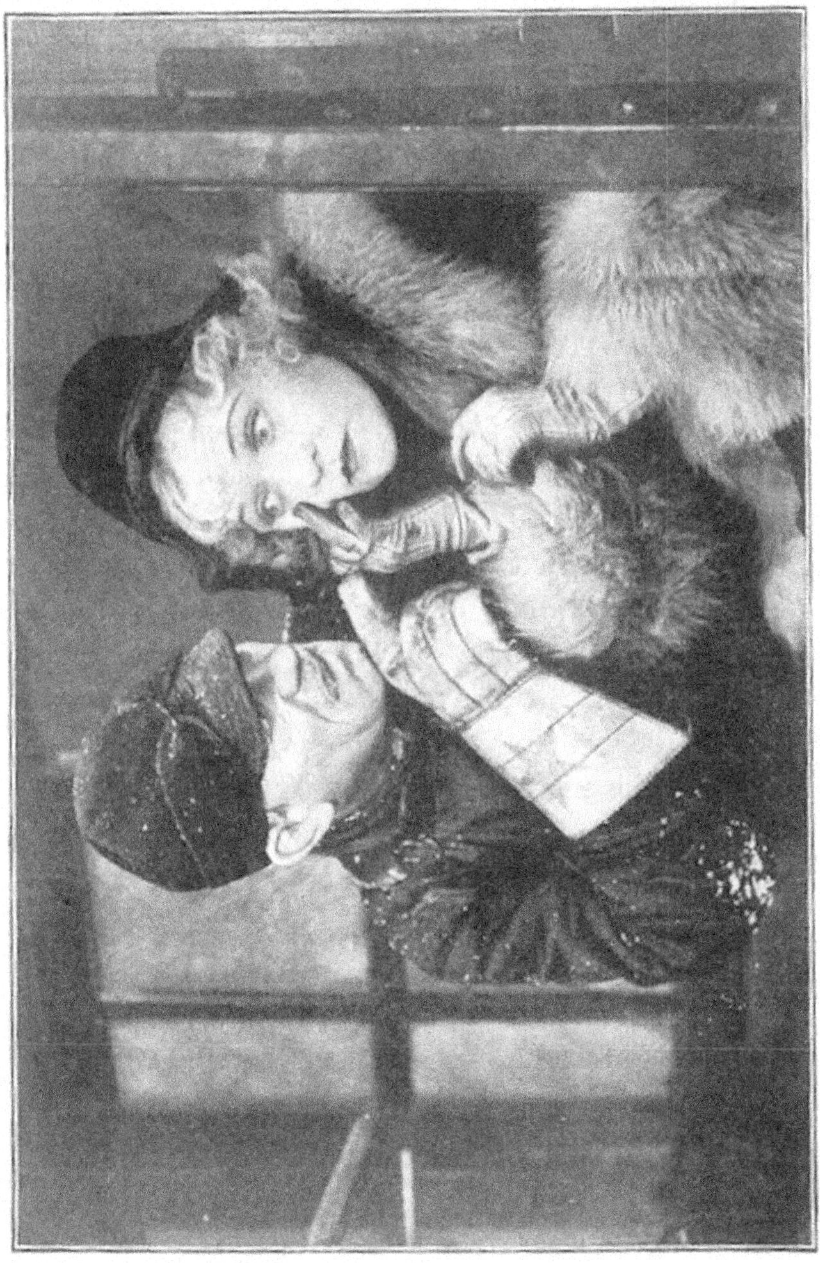

*"What are you looking at? You are pretty, like that"*

He was black as coal, smeared and dirty. This, no doubt, amused her and she, flirtatiously, powdered her nose with her fingertips.

Cheekily she pressed her lips back on the glass.

And he leapt to the smear it left from the other side.

They played their game in good fun, without giving anything of themselves.

But Grumpy reminded his driver not to get distracted from his duties. They were leaving, and the finish of their journey didn't look like it was going to be any brighter than the first part had been.

"Hello Tommy!"

Tommy, his fingertips covered with coal dust, took his leave and returned to his post. For a couple of minutes he had been wildly amused, a young boy, healthy and full of life.

On the locomotive, still eager to go, which exhaled plumes of hissing steam, where sparks broke free of the jaws of the devouring fire, Tommy had taken his place.

Tommy was fine. He lowered the pressure. A few shovelfuls of coal, a poke in the block glowing coal, and the monster roared again.

But shouts startled him.

It was his father who was shouting indignantly at the ground.

"Miss, I am not a taxi driver….If you are in a hurry, I am sorry. But you can't come up here…."

"I beg you Sir! My train is down here. It is imperative that I get to Chicago on time. I can only do that with you. You will not refuse me this! ...."

"Don't insist Miss, there is no place for you on my

locomotive...."

"I am very small..."

"The regulations forbid it. That's reason enough"

To cut short the conversation, the old man busied himself by greasing the links.

But suddenly, he turned

"Miss! I forbid you!"

And he pushed the beautiful beggar off the steps she had already climbed up.

"You are a cruel old man Sir!"

"Cruel or not, it's the same to me! But no! See these dolls? They think that everything is owed to them, that they have only to smile to break all the rules! ..."

"Dad! What do you care? .."

"Ah! What's it got to do with you, meddling"

Tommy recognized the little nostalgic traveler with whom he'd played a few seconds before. Meanwhile, she was not mistaken about the identity of her candid lover of a few minutes previously. And she gave him a tender look to intervene.

"But no!" Still grumbled Grumpy Anderson. "There's cause enough! The two of you...you make me do stupid things. Moreover, Shoo!!! We're leaving".

It seemed that a tear hung on the lashes of the unknown girl. It was perhaps a small drop attached to a flood of mascara.

Tommy rushed to her.

And during this Grumpy Anderson, amazed at his own audacity, took the young woman and threw her like a bundle of dirty linen to the bottom corner of the footplate.

"Don't move!"

"It's time!"

Not yet calmed down, Grumpy Anderson climbed onboard the engine. Opening the valves and pulling the levers. The train started.

The passenger took Tommy's hands, which he was hiding, and brought them to her lips. He was ashamed.

And yet he wondered suddenly if the unknown girl was so stressed because of real necessity. Was it so urgent for her to get to Chigaco? Men are generally smug, very young men are bound by conceit. Tommy was close to believing in love at first sight.

She had seduced him! She loved him! She would brave every danger to be with him! And, by God! What a conquest! Never had his clumsy hands raised so graceful and fragile burden. Never had such beautiful eyes implored him. Never!

His heart pounded in his chest, like it would burst. Too much pressure, really. If the engine had been like him it would never be late!

"The way, Tommy?"

"Clear, father!"

"Coal?"

"There you go!"

The snow continued to swirl and the icy wind bit at the faces of the two men. The storm had not ceased.

The passenger, half numb with cold, half roasted by the flames of the fire that ebbed with each new shovel load of coal, sore from being bumped, tossed from side to side, from one iron wall to another, began to find the situation unpleasant.

"Don't move!" advised a scared Tommy. "He'll not see you, especially!"

And he shielded her with his body.

"You are nice" she whispered to him.

He didn't hear, because in the roar of the engine she would have had to scream to be heard.

But suddenly she wasn't stood there anymore. She moved her place. And then the wrath of Grumpy Anderson would descend on her. A woman is never afraid of any man. Especially a beautiful woman. She knows she is the strongest.

Then away from Tommy, who wanted to avoid a scene, she got up and without him seeing, she approached the engineer

"Well, grandfather! You're stuck with me anyhow!."

"Oh!"

Old Grumpy couldn't utter a word, indignation choked him! How she was toying with him! There was a devil in this creature! Ah! How could this happen like that! .... for the first time on his locomotive, the rules were broken! ....

He looked at her with eyes both humble and fierce. He would have liked to throw her overboard. But at the same time he felt a sort of superstitious respect for her blatant audacity.

There was only one solution: to stop. He thought for a moment, and he was ready to push the lever ...

But the time was ticking away, implacable, second after second ....

And the delay had not been made up ....

Then he made a gesture of helplessness. Fate was

stronger than him. He resigned himself to the situation.

"Ah! It's swell, old thing!" she exclaimed, not wanting to risk his anger.

But in his bad mood, he pushes her roughly.

"Oh! He's still not nice, the old crab!"

And she went, as deftly as she could onto the unstable floor across from Tommy, whose eyes were full of joy.

"You can see very well that he has not eaten!"

The train now jumped as angrily as Grumpy himself. It seemed that the engine was matching the anger of its guide.

Abandoning his monitoring of the gauges, Grumpy Anderson suddenly cast a reproachful look at Tommy, reproachful and threatening

And the poor boy was caught between the desire to laugh and cry, because he knew his father well, and he was beginning to know the little lady who stood at his side.

She also had a strong head. The wind whipped her, made her disheveled. The cold froze her. She tried to cling on to anything. The sudden swaying of the engine as it took a curve rolled her into the coal. It did nothing to improve her humour.

She took a tiny mirror from her bag and looked at herself. She was all black and smeared with coal dust. She found this very funny.

Cheekily, she helped Tommy which made Grumpy angry again, when it seemed that he had forgotten about the control panel. It created a little collusion between her and the young man, which delighted him. And she enjoyed like crazy when the father, having caught on, yelled:

"The way?"

"Clear!"

"Coal! More coal!"

But now a miracle occurred. Suddenly, the face of Grumpy Anderson lost its severity. It was almost beaming

"Hello, Tommy!"

With his finger, the engineer indicated the time to his son. Victory! They had made up the lost time. They would enter the station exactly on time. Victory! Enormous pride swelled the old man's heart. Others would have flinched! An Anderson, never! All the obstacles had been overcome. They had triumphed over all, him and his engine .....

"That's swell that is!" she said.

"You, shut up, won't you! And hide" he added softly.

The station is announced in the distance by the multiplicity of signal lights, stretched into the night.

The bogies jumped as they crossed the first of the switches.

The pace is slowing.

Sweating and panting, like an athlete at the end of a run, the engine finally arrives at the platform.

The crowd rushed forward. The scurrying people, who had waited anxiously, as the notices had showed delays of several minutes, came to find their loved ones that Grumpy Anderson had delivered to their destination, in spite of all the obstacles.

The wheels slowed to a stop on the rails as Tommy forcefully applied the brake. He jumped down.

"Quick! Quick! Come on!"

His passenger bent down. He lifted her as if she were a straw and deposited her by his side. Then he looked at her without knowing what to say.

The important passengers were coming to congratulate and thank Grumpy Anderson. No one had dared to hope that everything would turn out well.

Grumpy Anderson himself couldn't believe it had all turned out well.

"On time is on time!" he replied simply, his ears still ringing.

With his great gloves in his hand, he gave a little oil to the wheels of the engine, like to a runner's body after a great effort.

Tommy was still looking at the girl. He feasted his eyes. If he had dared, he would, with a gesture, have spoken more eloquently . But he was shy.....

She laughed openly at his embarrassment.

"I am very grateful, you know."

"It's not worth mentioning!"

"But yes!! And I will thank your father."

Quietly, she approached the engineer and tapped him on the shoulder.

"What! You again!..."

"I've come to thank you!...."

"You have some nerve! ... Go! Where we don't have to see you! ... You are happy now? ... Okay! You are ... And have you seen yourself? ... You're pretty like this? ...Have a good time! Good evening."

She would not have supposed that the old man would be so spiteful.

"Well! Bah! It's not convenient you crab!"

But Tommy was back by her side.

"Miss, it's me who would like to thank you…"

"You are crazy…"

"My name's Tommy Anderson. And…."

"Hush!..."

"I would like to see you…."

"No kidding?..."

"You are so pretty…"

"Oh! I especially like that! Shouldn't you ask your father first? But still, I understand. Let's have fun. Come and see me. I'll be waiting for you…whenever you want."

Tommy rushed, took her small hand and kissed it.

"Be careful! You are all dirty"

Then rummaging in her bag:

"Here you are, my name and address!..."

And she fled, blowing a kiss from her fingertips.

"What are you looking at, son?"

"Oh! Nothing!..."

"Well! We will store the engine away and go. It's time to finish;"

"OK father"

They both went and uncoupled the locomotive. And while Grumpy Anderson let off the steam, Tommy hid in the small of his hand the little fragrant card which read:

Zella Maybelle,

Paralta Night Club

Telephone 86.

*Zella Maybelle, Paralta Night Club. Telephone 86.*

425-46

# CHAPTER III

The Anderson family was a family of railworkers. Grumpy lived with his son Tommy and his other son Jim, also employed by the North West Company. Jim was married and had a son, Davey, a super boy 5 years old, adored by all, but by his grandfather in particular.

They got along wonderfully, and the most perfect harmony reigned in this house where shared tastes and work formed a bond.

Grumpy and Tommy had arrived home. They were later than expected for dinner; but their meal was kept warm, simmering on the stove.

"Good evening Father!"

"Good evening Grandpa!"

"You're not too tired?"

"I am never tired". The father Anderson was solid as a rock and never tired, just like the engine that obeyed him.

He straightened up as he said this, in a sort of challenge.

Yet he felt a great weariness now he was home. The years, the bad weather, his advancing age, weighed heavily on his shoulders.

"Bad journey, huh?"

"Not at all! Why do you say that? A little bit of snow? It's like that every winter! It never prevents the wheels from rolling!"

While they took off their wet clothes, Molly, his daughter-in-law, set the table.

"You must be hungry?"

"Of course..."

It was Grumpy who had replied to this, and his was the place of honour at the table.

Tommy didn't feel the same.

"What's up son? You're not eating?"

"Yes, but..."

"Ta de da!....let's go! Don't dream. This is not the moment. Pile on the coal! Pile on the coal!"

"You know father, actually I am a little tired, and I'm looking forward to going to bed"

"I understand"

Grumpy adjusted his spectacles and read. But it was not just to pass the time. The habit of following a schedule filled up each and every minute until dinner. He did not agree with wasting even a relatively short time. And, he wouldn't want to be late for his coffee for anything in the world.

One day he had been surprised to find an excellent cake in the oven, specially made for him by his daughter-in-law, but because it was not the prescribed time to eat, he hadn't done so. In order to deceive, he had smeared a little cream on his lips...out of politeness and scruples.

Such was the man...and such were his beliefs, which were not so ridiculous!

The love of his work had become a passion. But passion doesn't always manifest itself in a normal rhythm.

"Here, father" said Jim. "There's a letter arrived for you"

"A letter!....who could want to write to me?..... where's it from?"

"From the Company"

"Quickly, give it to me"

Grumpy adjusted his spectacles and read. But, with the first few words his face darkened, and an expression of distress was painted on his face.

This was not the usual circular that all the engine drivers and firemen received!

'The Medical Board of the Company will meet at 3pm, next 15th January. All railworkers, firemen, drivers, conductors, brakemen and watchmen must be present to undergo a periodic medical examination as provided for in the Company regulations"

'Ah! Oh my!...They don't want much! Are we not strong and sturdy? Don't we see clearly? Do we have accidents?....Can't they leave us in peace?"

It was not, thank god, the first time that old Anderson had been invited to such an examination. But this was the first time he had vehemently railed against the institution.

Ah! The horror of getting old! And the cruel reminder of inevitable decline, year by year, when he still felt a strong will, a need of action, and, when all was said and done, a youngness of heart!....

It was good to remind himself of this, especially this evening, when he had done what no other could have done and where, despite everything, he had brought his train in safely AND on time.

He did not realize, perhaps, that he had driven with the help of Tommy's eyes, and that his unconscious temerity had, perhaps, obtained him a reward which he didn't merit.

"Ah! Oh my!" he grumbled again.

But little Davey climbed onto his lap.

"Say, grandpa, would you like to see what I was given today?"

"Show me"

"Here"

And the child brought a super miniature aeroplane, which, powered by a rubber band, he flew from one corner of the room to another.

"It's beautiful, huh?"

"It's a stupid toy"

"But it flies great!"

"It's ridiculous"

Seemingly, everything this evening was destined to annoy him.

"Put it away! Quickly! I have a much nicer toy to give to you"

"I don't understand" he added to the parents, "why you give a child such a machine"

He rose, and went down into the cellar.

From a hiding place where he had carefully concealed it, with caution, like a fragile piece of art, he took out a little locomotive and its tender. It was an absolutely faithful miniature reproduction of his actual engine "Thunder". How much work had gone into this toy!

Returning, he showed it off triumphantly.

"Here you go, my little Davey, a toy you should like more. Here, look"

Davey was happy to have something to play with. And, very attentively, he listened to his grandfather's instructions.

"You see, here.....when you pull this bar, you release the steam to run the box where the pistons are....so, it pushes the piston...and that acts on the connecting rod.... you see, it makes it move....and the wheels start to turn.... the train is going...."

"And the bell, grandpa?"

"The bell? You pull this string....After, when the train has got going, if you want it to go faster, you pull on the bar more and it makes more steam, and the piston is driven more quickly...You understand?....This, you see, this is the regulator....it prevents too much steam from going into the boilers at a given moment, and prevents the engine from exploding"

"Yours won't explode will it grandpa?"

"You are crazy! Has it ever had an accident with such a good driver? Has it ever had an accident with Grumpy Anderson? Here, these are the brakes.....when you have to stop suddenly because a signal is red. The steam is immediately cut. And this then brakes the cars, so they don't suddenly crash into you from behind"

"And this, grandpa?"

"That, it's the water pump"

"And this?"

"That's the speedometer..."

With great enthusiasm and great passion, Grumpy Anderson gave his explanations. He wanted to dissect this toy, to expose all its internal workings that he knew so well and looked after so well. His finger didn't indicate; it caressed as if the unfeeling metal toy was a living thing, sensitive, romantic.

"Come on Davey, time to say goodnight to Grandfather"

It was indeed bedtime.

Grumpy hugged the little boy whose eyes were starting to get heavy, contemplating, again, for a second, the little machine. Then he rose to put it away.

It seemed as he carried it, it was like cradling a newborn babe.

He would also go and lie down.

The day had been really tiring, moving almost, a day worth reckoning! He was happy it was over.

But that feeling made him think of Tommy, who he had almost forgotten about.

Poor boy! He was a brave guy! If he was asleep it was a good sign he was not too unwell.

"I'll go and say goodnight" he murmured.

He entered Tommy's room on his tiptoes, like a mother.

His son's work clothes had been thrown on a chair, in his hurry to get undressed quickly. He picked them up one by one and hung them in the wardrobe.

Would he go to bed and say goodnight? Under the sheets there was no movement. There was the shape of a body, unmoving, dead tired, crushed by sleep.

"Brave Tommy!" he said softly, patting his hand lightly on the covers.

And, in the darkness, he vanished silently.

To go to sleep, peacefully, serenely....

He could not guess, poor old fellow, that Tommy was far away, that in his bed was a dummy, improvised with clothes, a lure, a simple child's trick.

# Chapter IV

People did not go to Peralta Club to get bored! Certainly it was one of the most elegant establishments and the gayest in the city, one where you were sure to see the prettiest dancers and the most agreeable atmosphere.

The great hall, the floor shimmering, lights sparkling. Depending on the amount of makeup or healthiness, some faces were pale and others glowing. And the women supported the luster even more cheerfully, covering themselves with pearls or diamonds which enriched and embellished them.

“Well! Aren’t the girls coming back?” asked a jovial little fellow, becoming impatient, who believed, with the poet, that waiting to be happy becomes a suffering.

“They will soon” said his neighbor, who probably wanted to be patient himself.

“I came”, said the first, “for Zella Maybelle. I have been told she’s great!”

“She’s a pretty girl”

“Oh! An especially pretty girl...”

But here the orchestra struck up. A dance ! Here it is! The main attraction! ....

"Look! Here they are!..."

A troop of girls suddenly invaded the narrow space left free in the middle of the room, between the diners' tables. at a furious pace, they performed a few set movements, then opened their ranks, and there, carried aloft on a huge nest, covered with beautiful, plucked white birds feathers, emerged Zella Maybelle.

"Bravo! You weren't lying!" enthused the jovial little fellow, smacking his lips. This is a really nice touch".

The nest was laid on the ground, and Zella descended.

God thank you! The feathers adorning the veil barely covered her. Not her lovely shoulders or long legs nor her beautifully shaped thighs. The feathers, they were a decoy. They hid the fact she wore a slip and a bra ....

And here is the dancing. She danced the awakening of youth, the appeal of life, the joy of leaving the nest, pleasurable expectations, the hope of the future.

She danced with her whole being, her whole body, her whole heart, the intense pleasure of living, being healthy and beautiful, to offer.

She mimics the birth of love, its timidities, its toughness and its daring, its rashness. And finally, its fullness ....

It was a total delight, but a delight chaste, serene, simple and juvenile. Nothing was impure in itself, because it was very close to nature,full of rich images and emotions.

And her triumph was she was a woman in everything, and that held the promises of sincere and holy joy.

"Zella! ... Hey! ...."

Our little old man was hardly there for art. He didn't think with his emotions. He simply believed that Zella was particularly beautiful and desirable.

"Hey! .... Miss Zella! "

Thunderous applause swept the room. Breathless, Zelda bowed, sweeping the floor with her feathers, This daily ovation made her happy and was always new, and she was especially satisfied with herself.

Her girls entered the fray.

"Ah .... Well, that's nice, miss Zella, would you join me at my table. Champagne?" asked the old man.

"As you wish. But there's no chair here .... don't move ...."

And she sat on the lap of the little guy, bursting with happiness

"But be wise eh!" she said. "I sit here to keep an eye on my girls: it's not for your beautiful eyes, nor your bony knees ...."

"Flowers?"

"Of course! Gifts galore! ..."

"But hey! Hands off .... no, my boy! Champagne, flowers, as long as you want but that is touching, limpet! ... Besides, I must go! Goodbye!"

The girls, in fact, were on the last number of the program , kicking their legs, with a fixed smile on their lips, and in their hearts, the worry of being late for rendez-vous that they had fixed with their boyfriends.

"Miss", Zella's dresser said to her when the star of Paralta entered her dressing room, "There is a you man who is asking to see you".

"A young man? Do I know him?"

"No doubt! But me, I've never seen him before. He didn't want to give his name.....He simply instructed me to say does Miss remember being on a train journey, on the locomotive."

"Ah!....Ah yes! That journey. Ah! if you only knew, my dear .... Exceedingly funny! .... And how was the young man? .... A beautiful boy, with brown hair and eyes full of laughter?....Huh?..."

"Oh, you know.....A young man like all the others...."

"Blockhead!"

The maid pinched her lips, vexed.

"It is possible, Miss, that I am. Anyway, this gentleman told me that he would ... And besides ..."

"What? ..."

"Here …"

Timidly opening the door of the dressing room, all red with embarrassment, a man entered.

"Miss Zella Maybelle?"

"That's me"

"Oh! Miss!......."

"My dear Tommy!..."

"You see, Miss Zella .... It might be too bold ... But I have not lost a minute and here I am ..."

"It's lovely to see you .... You've been so kind!"

Conversation followed. Tommy was hardly used to these kinds of meetings. Sitting on the edge of a chair in the dressing room-boudoir, full of flowers, the atmosphere was heavy with strange perfumes and fragile ornaments, he stood awkwardly. It was so different to

*He noticed that they were eating outside the prescribed time.*

*"Here my little Dave, a toy that will please you more."*

*"Say, grandpa, do you see what they gave me today?"*

*They did not come to the Paralta Club to be bored.*

the fresh air he breathed while driving the locomotive! …

Zella Maybelle broke the silence:

"I hoped you would come. But I did not expect you back so soon. It was just a few hours ago that we got off this happy train that saved the day for me .... where I had the pleasure to meet you ...."

"The pleasure, Miss, was all mine...."

"Go on! You little flatterer!.... But by what miracle are you already here, looking like a gentleman, when I've barely left you, coal black and in a disgusting state?"

"It's very simple! I went home with my father and, at dinner time, I pretended to be tired and go to bed..... While old Anderson and the family ate, I got washed up, changed my clothes and climbed out of the window, my shoes in my hands, after having made a dummy which I slid into my bed..."

"Well! That's love if I'm not mistaken! Love at first sight, what?"

Tommy hung his head and didn't reply. He turned as red as a poppy.

"Brave Tommy, go!" Teased Zella patting his cheeks. "I was not expecting this visit, your visit .... and that's why I am having much more fun. But you're not too tired?"

"Oh! Not at all!..."

"Then you'll come with me?"

"If you'll permit it?"

"On bended knees..."

But she broke out laughing, ruining his spontaneity.

With this free-spirit, which is not immodesty, but instead indicates confidence in purity and camaraderie, Zella Maybelle took off her make-up and washed herself without causing a scene.

She had removed the light and almost paradoxical costume feathers before the mirror, rubbing the feathers with a white fat.

Tommy said nothing, but he looked at her greedily, as a thirsty man contemplates a source of water, and his confusion made him blush

She was there, beside him, without vanity, without self-consciousness, as if he did not exist. She had bare legs, long legs, slender, beautifully modeled, which made him nervous and full of impatience. Her beautiful arms were bare too, and her shoulders, smooth and curved where she wore her hair. Her back was bare and sleek. And nothing concealed her breasts, twin glories, her breasts firm and pearly, full of youth and life. Ah! as Tommy, with trembling palms despaired, he imagined a breastplate, a shield, a veil ....

Suddenly turning, she caught the curiosity of the young man, and she did not think badly or feel ashamed.

"Oh, I beg your pardon! " she said.

And she ran to hide in the small bathroom that was formed by a curtain drawn across one corner of her dressing room.

There, the kid in her returned, and her pearly laughter trilled out.

"Well! Tell me something now, Mr. Tommy ...."

But Tommy did not answer.

Now that she was no longer there,under his gaze, he felt even more emotional. Because, now, he could imagine. He followed the progress of her small bare feet, visible under the hem of the curtain. And he delighted in his imagining of an endearing image. Absent and discreetly hidden, she was at this instant a thousand times more naked than before.

She reappeared in a moment.

This time, he would not swear that there was something wrong with her coquetry. Certainly, there was nothing untoward in her outfit. her legs were sheathed in silk and she didn't lack for her dress. But she knew, without doubt, the power of her charms and dapper dress, which concealed, like a pistol, its exquisite femininity.

"Viola! Another instant and I will be ready"

There was a knock at the door.

"Come in!"

She turned:

"Hi! It's you, Jimmy!" she said in a dry tone.

"Hello beautiful!'

A young man entered.

He was well dressed. He had the air of somewhat insolent master, or the least favorite. Probably also the vanity of his money.

He looked offended that Tommy did not move from his chair, and then, as if to gauge him, shot him an imperceptible protective greeting.

"Well! Zella! You're not ready yet? I thought that you didn't want to make me wait nevertheless".

"What are you doing?'

"I'm taking you to supper"

"Oh! It's impossible this evening"

"Sorry? You promised me yesterday. There is no impossibility that counts. I am waiting and I will take you".

"You're talking out of the top of your head".

"Top of my head huh?" he sneered. And sitting down, he continued: "I'm waiting for you"

"Jimmy, please, leave me alone this evening....Forgive me...Let's have our supper tomorrow. This evening is impossible, believe me".

"Ah! And what's his name, this impossible?"he scoffed.

"You're being rude"

"Some nerve! You insult me now? Get away with you my little Zella, I'm not the villain here'

"Oaf!"

Jimmy paled. He felt a cold anger rising. But he controlled himself, and said, very sweetly: "I understand, my love, you're still not ready. I hear you, I'm going to busy myself."

And he sat down in an armchair, his feet on a chair on which were hanging Zella's gloves.

"You see, I am very happy to wait for you.... and I do not despair of taking you to my little supper ... with a slight delay .. It will be better."

"Go away!" shouted Zella.

Exasperated, she glared at him.

"Go away! Leave me alone!"

"Now, put your coat on...."

Tommy got up in an instant. Prowling gently into the small room, turning his cap in his hands, not knowing what to do.

Who was this man who spoke with such arrogance and acted like a master? Something that felt like a vague jealousy stirred in his heart. And he suffered to see the graceful Zella helpless against the cruelties of this pretentious lout.

"Go away! ... or I'll scream!" .... the young woman shouted one last time. And her eyes went round the boudoir, as if seeking assistance. It was not long in coming! Distraught at her distress, finally freeing the waves of his anger long restrained, Tommy jumped. The man sprang forward. But too late. Tommy dodged the first blow. Then his fist shot towards the jaw of his opponent, and in a crash of overturned tables, trinkets rolled at his feet.

With all the commotion people had appeared. But an exasperated Tommy was straight onto them. Possessed by a destructive rage, he rushed at the first man who entered and his fists fell again. His strength felt increased tenfold. Another body went down next to Jimmy's.

"Tommy! Tommy!" yelled Zella Maybelle, both happy and scared at the same time.

Tommy didn't hear her, he heard nothing. Then she took him by the hand.

At the door a third adversary tried to bar their way. Tommy punched him on the shoulder and jostled him into the hallway......

"Tommy! Come quickly! Come quickly!...."

She led him, running, through a maze of corridors.

They descended the dizzying stairs, still hand in hand, past the artists' dressing rooms, until finally they were on the street where the icy cold sobered them up.

"Quick Tommy!"

Zella's car was at the entrance. She jumped behind the wheel. He got in and sat next to her.

They drove off into the night. Without doubt, his head was full of emotions. They didn't talk.

"You're a nice guy Tommy" she murmured to him.

When the excitement had passed, each sat lost in their own thoughts.

Zella was embarrassed.

"What must he think of me?" she thought to herself.

How could he understand that a man could enter my room and speak to me like he was my master, believing he had the right to do it. How he must judge me!

And she was somewhat frightened by what he'd done, his audacity and his anger. How could he, in cold blood, been able to lose his head that way?

But what was the good in thinking?

Though she might be a little worried, she felt a secret pleasure to have found a young man who was willing to do so much for her, and with such valour, her very own knight in shining armour!

His simplicity, his spontaneity, his embarrassment even, were a change from so many of her other companions!

Tommy felt the warmth of her body against him. A body that he admired, an adorable little body that he would never dare touch with his rough hands. But oh!, what delight in this light contact!

"We've arrived Tommy!"

The car stopped in front of an illuminated garage where a chauffeur waited. They got out.

"Would you give me your arm until I reach my door?"

There were 10 metres to the door.

Tommy took the arm of the artiste. He didn't accompany her, as much as almost carry her. He didn't want her silver shoes splashed with mud, her little feet tired with walking.

"Tommy, thank you so much. You were very nice to me this evening. And I am really happy to have seen you"

Then she became her usual cheerful self, seeming to remember how the young engine driver had come into her life, she added:

"But I would like to also see your father Anderson!"

"Oh! But he will not come to see you!"

"Really? Ah well! Then I must come to your home..."

"You....you...come to our home?"

"But why not?"

"Oh!..." It was the only answer Tommy could give, so strong was his joy!

"The day after tomorrow if you'd like?...I work really hard....I'll invite myself to dinner at your home..."

"Miss....that's wonderful....I'm really happy...."

"But, at least give me your address!"

She opened the door of her house. In the doorway Zella handed Tommy her little notebook in which he wrote down for her the necessary information.

"So miss, you really mean it?"

"Of course! I said so didn't I, kid?"

He took off his hat and, holding out his hand, waited.

"Ah well! Goodbye Tommy! Go to sleep and dream....."

"Good night Miss"

Then, with one last glance, as if he wanted to make the image last forever, he turned, descended the steps and walked through the garden.

She had remained in the doorway, watching him leave.

As he walked away he turned to wave goodbye.

"Tommy! Tommy!" she called to him.

"Miss?"

He hurried back.

"Haven't you forgotten something?"

"No...I don't think so..."

"Really?"

"But I....I..."

'Have a good look at me..."

She leaned towards him....

He hesitated for a moment, then rushed towards her.

"Ah! You see...." she started to say.

But she got no further as Tommy kissed her, then took flight.

"Goodbye Tommy!"

"Goodbye Zella!"

# Chapter V

Tommy Anderson had his sister-in-law Molly as a counsellor and confidante.

The only woman in the house, she was obliged to take on other roles than simply that of wife and mother. She was a little sister to Tommy and a daughter to Grumpy.

"Feeling better Tommy?" she asked the next morning, seeing her brother-in-law reappear. "I was worried when you went to bed without any dinner. It's true you had had a very hard journey and were really tired"

"Oh! That's all passed!"

"But this morning you are positively glowing!"

"Is that so?"

"You recovered quickly"

"That's because I wasn't ill..."

"How so?"

"Yes...yes...it was an excuse. Nobody knew what I was up to. But, last night, I wasn't in my bed.....at least not all night..."

'What is this? This story?"

"Come, sit down for a while next to me Molly. I must tell you. You asked me about my health just now, and you were ecstatic about my current state. Ah well! I was absolutely fine last night, but today I am sick!"

"In other words?..."

"Yes!"

"And this illness?"

"I believe that I am in love Molly!"

"Great news! This is a sickness that is not dangerous! And it's about time at your age! But with who?"

"Ah well!....You know, or you don't know, she's the one I brought back yesterday evening on the locomotive..."

"Bugger! It's love at first sight!.."

"Hush!...I brought back a pretty passenger despite my father's opposition...but I brought her onboard without his knowledge. And he didn't have the time to get rid of her because he couldn't afford to lose one second. We were already really delayed..."

"I understand...your father and his timekeeping!..."

"She was pretty like a sweetheart, and kind...when she got off the train, she told me it would be a pleasure to see me again and she gave me her address"

"And you rushed to her as fast as your feet could carry you...you didn't lose any time..."

"You see!"

"This pretty passenger, what does she do?"

"She's called Zella...isn't that a pretty name?...she's an artiste. She dances every evening at the Paralta Club"

"Hmmm!"

"Why do you say hmmm?"

"I don't know...It seems to me that a dancer and a locomotive driver....you know....I fear you are making up a beautiful dream"

"I'm also afraid when I have these feelings...it occurs to me that it's impossible...And yet, she knows me...I didn't deceive her"

"You are a handsome and kind man Tommy!"

"However, here's the thing, I saw her yesterday evening and she told me she wants to come and see papa Anderson. She is coming tomorrow evening, as soon as we have our dinner"

"You're crazy! Bringing her here! How's she getting here?"

"By car"

"She has a car, and you think that..."

"It was her who told me that she is inviting herself to dinner with us"

"Ah well! My boy, that's very generous of her!"

"It bothers you? I should have consulted you first of course..."

"But no, it doesn't bother me, rather it's a pleasure. But I don't like surprises"

"I will tell her no then, she is easy and....adorable"

"You mean you love her..."

"Even if I didn't love her..."

"I understand Tommy. We will welcome your beautiful girl the best way we can. But your father, what will he say??"

"Papa! You must not warn him!"

"Perfect. Now leave me to prepare the soup"

Davey, his little nephew, had come to take his place with his mother.

"Tell me Uncle, why does grandpa not want me to play with the aeroplane that you gave me?"

"But Davey, your grandpa understands only one thing: the railways"

"But the plane, it's very fast!"

"It's because of this, he thinks it's dangerous'

"People don't get killed by railways?"

"No...finally...you understand....it's less dangerous because people don't fall from a great height..."

"Ah! So grandpa would like that I would be an engine driver..."

"No! No! Never...."

He shouted this out without thinking. He quickly recovered his composure.

"You are very small Davey. You have time to grow up and think about what you will do later. There are more things in life than railways..."

"You don't want to tell me a story Uncle?"

"I don't know any"

"If not...make one up!"

"You think that's easy!"

"Tell me a fairy tale!"

"There are no more tales, Davey!"

"It doesn't matter!"

"Bugger!...Ah well! Wait...I will think of one, a really nice one...there!...listen...Once upon a time there was a young man who had black hands, who spent his whole life in the coal, and who wore dirty clothes..."

"That was an engine driver, I guess"

"Don't interrupt me like that!...One day, he lives next to the prettiest girl he has ever seen, with hair full of sunshine, a skin white like the snow and hands so fine they could be flowers"

"And what does she say to him, the pretty girl of the snow?"

"She says to him: I love you..."

"That's all?"

"That's all"

"But that doesn't finish like all the other stories. They always say "they were married, lived happily ever after and had lots of children", isn't that so?"

"Why, I adore you Davey!"

Tommy hugged the child and got up.

Old Grumpy Anderson entered.

"Hello Dad!"

"Well, you're doing better? You were sleeping well last night when I came to check on you in your room. It wasn't serious then?"

"No, as you can see"

"Tell me Molly, what time will dinner be ready? We need to be at work at 3:53pm. It's now 11:57am. In 6 minutes exactly on the table!"

"I'm hurrying!"

"Bah!" said Tommy, "Why does it have to be 12.03 exactly? If it's a little later we can just eat a little quicker!"

"No, my son! We won't eat a little quicker. We will eat on time. To respect time is our religion here! You have never seen me do anything a second later when it could be done immediately. Our profession demands that. And, because our life is so well regulated, our profession is the most wonderful of all, the profession that my father did, that my son does, and that my grandson will do"

"And that he will enjoy?" asked Molly.

"Ah! No, not if you let him play with that damned aeroplane....but now it's 12.03! Let's eat!"

Grumpy Anderson sat down. At that moment there was nothing more important in the world to grandfather than his lunch.

He was installed in his chair as if he was at the controls of his engine entering the station, right on schedule!

Tommy, although he had been raised in the rough schooling of his father, although he had heard him sing the splendors of his profession a thousand times and the nobility of his job, did not exactly share in his father's enthusiasm.

His was a generation that accepted less and less restraint, and for who this time was the most intolerable.

He would gladly be pleased with his father if he did not fear his anger. But his Dad was, with his special sense of duty, an excellent father, and his authority was recognized by his son. That he sometimes became manic could be excused, since his mania was harmless.

Tommy, however, couldn't stop himself from intervening.

"It's possible we should always live by a schedule. But I don't consider it the be all and end all"

"On the contrary....A time that has passed cannot be relived. Everything is measured. Everything takes place as it should and as it was planned. Time is the order.

And order is the fundamental quality of life. Reflect on that Tommy!"

"Yes, but....where's the fascination in life? Waiting for tomorrow, if you know it will be like today?"

"I only ask that it will be like yesterday"

"And imagination?"

"Imagination? But I exclude that from my life! It has no place there. I don't expect anything from it, except things I don't wish for! I believe, my dear Tommy, that you'd rather try to follow your imagination. Unhappily! Do you know where that will lead you? No! Our lives are calm and happy because they are timed, because there is a time for every thing, and every thing has its time... Indeed, you must feel this. But you arc young, you will learn"

"So, I'm not allowed to question anything until I'm older?"

"Fool!"

Grumpy Anderson thereupon took out his watch and jumped up.

"It's time! One second more and we would have been late! Come on Tommy! Get ready! We have to leave for work!"

"Goodbye grandpa!"

"Goodbye little Davey! Have fun...with the locomotive!"

The two men went into their rooms to change into their work clothes. But before doing so, Tommy reminded Molly about the coming evening.

"Say, Molly, you'll let Jim know"

"Yes of course"

"Tell him it will be our great pleasure to welcome her"

"You know very well that your brother loves you alot. Don't worry. We will make an effort to soften your father. Now, go!"

"Goodbye Molly! You are an angel"

"And she is wonderful!"

"You are jealous"

"Go! Get gone! Good luck. Don't tire yourself too much. And don't think too much about her on the journey, so you can see the signals clearly!"

"You can be sure"

Outside the voice of his father rose:

"So Tommy! Are you coming? It's 1:22pm. We always leave at this time!"

Tommy made a gesture of exasperation..

"Ah! Him and his minutes!.....what century is he in?"

Then he rushed out.

"OK Dad, I'm all yours!"

*...there appeared, carried aloft, a huge nest, from which emerged Zella.*

*Zella was covered with white feathers, resembling a magnificent bird*

*"Ah! And how do you call this? Your impossibility?"*

# Chapter VI

Grumpy Anderson, although he wouldn't admit it, most of all to himself, was beginning to feel the effects of the tremendous workload of being the driver of a major express train.

He had been doing the job for years. He didn't remember ever having had any worries about it. He had always given his all to his work.

And now, wanting to hold on, despite his age, wanting, as far as possible, to hold back that fatal retirement, he stiffened his muscles and his will. But his shoulders were stooping. And his brooding and bitter thoughts became dark and melancholy.

He should be cheerful tonight however. He was home with his whole world around him. Tommy was off duty at the same time as him. It felt so good to be in a soft, warm home, when the cold was raging outside, and after hours of enduring the biting frost and cold, blowing wind.

It was then that Davey came with his little locomotive, seeking some technical explanation from the old man.

"See my little fellow, it's not surprising that it doesn't work.....if you don't loosen your brakes before getting up steam how do you expect it to pull so many tons?"

"So, I must turn this?"

"But no, that's where the water comes. Here....you turn the wheel like this"

'Ah, OK grandpa....say grandpa, won't you tell me a story?"

"Ask your mother"

"But grandpa, you are very old, you must know more....."

"I tell you I don't...leave me alone..."

"Well. I'm going to tell you one..."

"No kidding?!"

"Yes...once upon a time there was a man like you, who was a train driver, and one day a girl who was as beautiful as the snow and the sun, said to him "I love you" and they had lots of children....you see?"

"That's a completely silly story!"

"No grandpa"

"And why not, if you please?"

"Because it is the story of my uncle Tommy!"

His mother who was there, quickly intervened:

"Say, Davey, first of all you must not say no to your grandfather when he says yes. Secondly, don't tell silly stories which we don't know"

"Me, I tell what I know Mama!"

"Hush, hush!" said Grumpy Anderson.

"It's not a question of that. He tells lots of stories

but he never believes them. There was never a woman who came onboard the train to marry the driver. It cannot happen. It should not happen. And, furthermore, it is absolutely forbidden to allow strangers to come aboard the locomotive. Do you understand?..."

But the brat clung to his idea.

"It is true! Since my uncle told me this yesterday!"

"Ah! So!"

Had he?...This wasn't possible....And yet!.....Grumpy Anderson suddenly remembered the little woman who had evaded his vigilance an who he had brought to Chicago. A beautiful liability! The first, the only and certainly the last! He wanted to forget, at all costs, this breach of the rules that endured in his memory. And here he was, reminded of it!....A beautiful girl who said "I love you" to the driver...what nonsense!

But surely Tommy would not confuse illusion with reality, not even accidentally? He was nevertheless a serious boy, thoughtful......No, it wasn't possible.

Ten times he returned to his chair. He wanted to call Tommy and ask for an explanation. But it seemed so improbable that he was afraid of being ridiculous.

"Enough of this nonsense Davey. Bring me your locomotive"

"Here you are grandpa"

"I will explain to you. Here, you see, this is the place for the engine driver who is in charge, here is the place for his assistant who obeys his commands. And you see, there is not another place. There is no place for pretty girls who love the driver, and who don't exist"

"You've seen the news, father?" said Jim, handing

him the newspaper he'd just been browsing.

"It's not yet the time for me to read"

"Well"

"Where is Tommy?"

"He's taking some fresh air outside the door"

"This is not the time to take fresh air! It's freezing cold. He'll catch his death of cold. He's crazy...Get in here Tommy!"

"You called me father?"

"Yes, Tommy. You aren't very sensible. Don't stay outside, just standing there, in this weather"

"I'm not cold"

"It doesn't matter...but tell me, what are you doing there?"

"What?"

"There, with that tooth pick"

"I am cleaning my fingernails"

"You are doing your nails!...Ah! Don't make me laugh!...You handle coal. And now you are making a manicure?! What next, are you going to paint them?!"

"It's not necessary to be dirty to be a good worker"

"OK! So we are dirty, so what? But when you clean with such meticulousness, it means you begin to be afraid of getting dirty, that you are embarrassed to get dirty... Are you ashamed of being an engine driver by chance?"

"If I were ashamed I wouldn't do it"

"Gee! So, go and do like the others! Say, Jim, now it's time. Pass me the newspaper"

# CHAPTER VII

Tommy did not take his seat. Just returned, it appeared, he was plagued by that anxiety common to all lovers. It was not yet time for her to arrive. Even so, he waited anxiously. And with each passing second a doubt was born in his mind.

She wasn't going to come!

Was she just toying with him? Had she already forgotten him? Was her promise just some trivial politeness made on the spur of the moment?

He didn't want to believe that this was the case. It was not really the truth. He didn't want his doubts to grow like a malignant tumor.

But he could not help thinking the worst/

Were there not any repercussions of the scandal he had caused the day before? After a moment of madness, did she realize she was committing a folly, that she would never want to spend time with a guy who was a train driver, her who wore such expensive jewelry, and at whose golden feet men knelt?

To give himself courage, he closed his eyes and tried to remember the exquisite taste of the kiss she had given him on her doorstep. That, at least, could not be poisoned by lies.

"Well! Aren't we eating tonight?" said Grumpy Anderson, folding his newspaper.

"But yes of course father!"

"We should already be at the table, and nothing seems ready"

"It's going to be"

"Molly, I don't recognise you anymore! You are usually so punctual. What has happened today?"

Behind him, Jim and Tommy smiled. He turned around and caught them by surprise.

"So what are you all up to? Caught red handed my dears! Spending your time running from the hallway to the door, the dinner is late, and I turn round to find you making fun of me. Why? What's going on?"

"Grandfather" said Molly, with a wink to her brother-in-law, "We are waiting for a guest for dinner"

"Ah! Ah! And who is this guest?"

"A girl!"

"A girl? What girl?"

Tommy blushed, then said:

"Father, it's the young traveller who we gave a lift to the other day, when the weather was so bad and our train was running late...."

"I made up for that lateness!" interrupted Grumpy.

"She wanted to come and thank you"

"She needn't thank me. I wasn't authorised to have her onboard"

"She asked us to let her come..."

"I don't want to see her..."

"Don't be mean father"

"If that girl comes to my house, I'm going"

"You wouldn't do that" said Molly "you are not so mean as you pretend to be. And perhaps she is really nice, this visitor..."

"I.."

At that moment they heard the sound of a car horn. Tommy rushed to the door. Outside it was beginning to get dark. But he recognized, straight away, her silhouette getting out of the car.

"You!"

"Of course me" she joked. "You're surprised to see me? You weren't waiting for me? I should turn back?"

"Zella!"

"Hush...I have come to see papa Anderson. Is he here?"

"Yes, but..."

"Never mind the 'but', I must go and kiss him hello!"

And she headed towards the house, hopping to avoid the puddles.

It was like the day she had come to ask for a place on the locomotive, mischievous, playful, gay, very simply dressed, like a little girl. And she did not seem to worry too much about the presence of Tommy, who followed, a little sad that he had not had the welcome he had hoped for and which he had imagined.

"Good evening!"

Molly and Jim had come to the door. Tommy introduced them:

“My brother and my sister-in-law. My little nephew Davey”

“Oh! He’s so cute!”

“Miss Zella Maybelle, a great artiste!”

“Say you! Am I paying you for my publicity?! But where is good old father Anderson?”

“He is there” said Molly, “behind his newspaper”

“Good evening father Anderson”

Old Grumpy didn’t raise his eyes.

“Don’t pay any attention” whispered Molly in her ear,”this evening he’s being really gruff”

She made a gesture to say ‘it’s no big deal’, and she repeated:

“Good evening father Anderson”

Same failure, no response.

“Oh! But he doesn’t look comfortable!”

She walked behind him, and leaned over to touch his hair, and shouted into his ear:

“Good...evening...Mis...ter...An..der...son...”

“What? What? What is this?...Good evening Miss. But why have you come here?”

“At this time? Why for dinner I should think!”

“I didn’t invite you”

“I think that your children are much more nicer than you...”

“Bah!”

And with that he plunged back into reading the latest news.

“Father Anderson, if you do not put down your newspaper, I am going to get angry!”

“Leave me in peace!..”

"Oh! Not on your life...I want to see you laugh..."

"Ah well! You will not see that!"

And furiously, Grumpy stormed into the next room.

"It's true" confessed Zella. "For an easy going guy he is not so accommodating!"

But already she was busy, lively, gay, vivacious.

"Ah! I am so happy to know you all! I was so happy, two days ago, that Tommy kindly took me onboard the locomotive..."

"It was the least I could do Miss"

"My name is Zella. I want everyone to call me Zella. Is that understood?!"

"Sure"

"And I don't want to be useless! I want to help Molly. I am very good around the kitchen. What are you making there? It smells really good. Let me taste it"

"Oh! You know, I don't think it's ready yet!"

"OK, you don't need help I see! But come with me for a little while my little Davey. You are charming....He is very well behaved for such a little one. And he looks like his grandfather most vividly!"

A cough in the next room, followed by the impatient voice of Grumpy:

"Davey! Davey! Come here..."

But Davey was in no hurry to go to his grandfather.

Grumpy then appeared in the room.

"Miss, it is time for the little one to eat. Don't make him late"

"Don't worry I will make sure he has his dinner. If you don't mind that is?"

"It's for me to give him his dinner" said Grumpy.

"Well it's up to Davey of course who gives him his dinner"

It was obvious to old Anderson that he didn't have the upper hand. It would be in vain to try and grab the kid.

Zella sat opposite him. And it was obvious the child found the company of this pretty girl, with her soft skin and nice smell, very agreeable, and it would have been too bad to separate them.

"It's all good!" he said, "Let's eat!"

Zella and Davey had straight away become best friends in the world.

"Are you going to tell me a story Miss?..."

"In a little while. Eat now"

After dinner Davey brought a big cake to Zella.

"You don't like it better with cream?" asked Grumpy Anderson.

"No grandpa"

"Good, so I will eat it all myself"

But Davey scoffed at this and cared little that his grandfather had the whole cake.

When it came time to put the child to bed, the same comedy occurred.

"It's my job" said grandfather.

"But Davey prefers that I put him to bed tonight"

"I give the orders here Miss"

"You will obey me Sir!"

Were they going to cut poor Davey in two, like they were Solomon?!

Finally it was Grumpy who soothed the situation a little, though he did so with great reluctance! No, really, this girl, she was a nightmare! Her mere presence was an accusation of weakness or cowardice...he sensed there was something about her he could not be happy with... He didn't agree to this dinner with his children. He hoped for the time to pass quickly.

But the meal was not less jolly for this.

"It's the first time" said Zella "that I have seen a good decent man succeed for so long to pretend to be wicked. Too bad for him!"

"Our father" said Jim, "Has always been somewhat eccentric. But now he is especially annoying. He must go to have a medical examination by the Company. And he fears that he will no longer be able to keep his locomotive"

"And if that were to happen, he would die" added Tommy, "Like a fish out of water. My father lives for his engine, it is his life...."

"You don't share his passion?"

"Ah! Certainly not!..."

And in that instant, Tommy, silently, realized he was a dreamer

"I am not bored by your company...but I have to go, you know! I also have my job to do....and I can't keep the Paralta Club waiting"

"Already!"

"I regret it more than you. It's lovely here...and you are all so nice...even the old crab!"

They laughed.

"Me also" said Jim, "It's time for me to leave too. My work starts in an hour"

"Oh! I pity you, in this cold!"

"Bah! It's our job"

Jim left the dining-room, to go and put on some warm clothes, stopping for a moment at the foot of the cradle where his little boy slept, then, having lit a storm lamp, he reappeared.

"Here I am! Ready!"

"Goodbye Molly!"

"Goodbye Jim. And be careful!"

"Goodbye my dear wife"

"Goodbye Miss"

Outside the cold had become more intense and the snow was freezing. He slipped at every step.

"Wait Miss Zella. The path is dangerous. I will carry you"

Jim and Tommy joined their hands and Zella, laughing out loud, jumped onto the improvised seat.

"Here's an entrance I should have for the Paralta!"

Between the pair of them, they carefully put her into her car.

Then Jim waved, took the small path that went to the station, which he could just about see far away in the cold light, and disappeared.

Tommy stayed there, near to the car door.

"Do you remember, Tommy, that day we kissed, without knowing, on both sides of the car window?"

"Oh! Yes..."

"And you would like to do it again?"

"I think so..."

In a flash, she closed the car door.

Straight away Tommy pressed his lips against the glass.

But, smiling, she lowered the window.

And their warm lips, alive and vibrant, pressed together.

"Oh! Zella!"...Again!..."

For a long time, without holding each other, they drank each others breath.

"You love me Zella?"

"You big fool! Would I be here if I hated you?"

"And will you always love me Zella?"

"We must never speak of tomorrow...isn't today enough for you?"

"Bye for now Zella!"

She pressed the starter button on her car. The engine turned over.

She put her little hand on Tommy's warm mouth.

"I take a kiss from you for later...You see that I am a glutton!"

"Zella! Zella!"

The car sped off. Its lights soon disappeared. Tommy waited for a moment, dazzled at being so close to his love.

# CHAPTER VIII

A very painful task, and one which the good, decent Jeff wanted to be free of. But he had been told:

"Old fellow, you are a longtime friend of Grumpy Anderson. You will know best how to explain this to him. Perhaps he will suffer less if you tell him"

"It is still a rough chore" he thought to himself.

How was he going to break this tragic news? What words could he find?

Alas! He felt too much sorrow himself to hide his expression of grief.

And when he arrived in front of the locomotive shed, where he knew Grumpy was preparing to depart, he stood there hesitating for what seemed an eternity.

Finally, finding a young coal loader, he simply said:

"Go tell Grumpy Anderson that his old mate Jeff is waiting for him at the door with something important to tell him..."

How was he going to tell him?

Anderson appeared. He looked worried.

"What's up Jeff? What do you want?"

"My poor friend!" Jeff said simply. And he burst into tears, wringing his hands.

"A misfortune has happened?""a really great one..."

"But to who?...Jim?..."

"Have courage Grumpy!"

"What!...He's dead?.."

Jeff didn't reply.

"But it's not possible!...He left the house this evening to go to work...He was happy..healthy..strong...It's not possible!...It can't have ended in disaster..."

"Unhappily!"

Grumpy Anderson wavered. It seemed as if he were going to fall into a heap. But he stiffened himself. He furiously wiped away the tears from his eyes, surprised, perhaps, that they were the first he had ever shed.

"Jeff, tell me what happened"

"It's like this: Jim had come to work and had to go with train 1149 But at the signal, the convoy didn't start. The ice had frozen the brakes. The wheels were locked. So Jim jumped on the roof of one of the wagons, then another, jumping from one to another, releasing the breaks. He had freed the last wagon and was climbing down when the convoy suddenly started. He staggered. His shoes didn't have a grip on the ice which covered the roofs. He slid and fell off the side...Just then, an oncoming train...."

"Poor Jim!...And he said nothing?"

"No! It was over so quickly!...Before he fell, he was shouting at his laughing colleagues: "you can say to my father that, thanks to Jim, a blocked train would depart

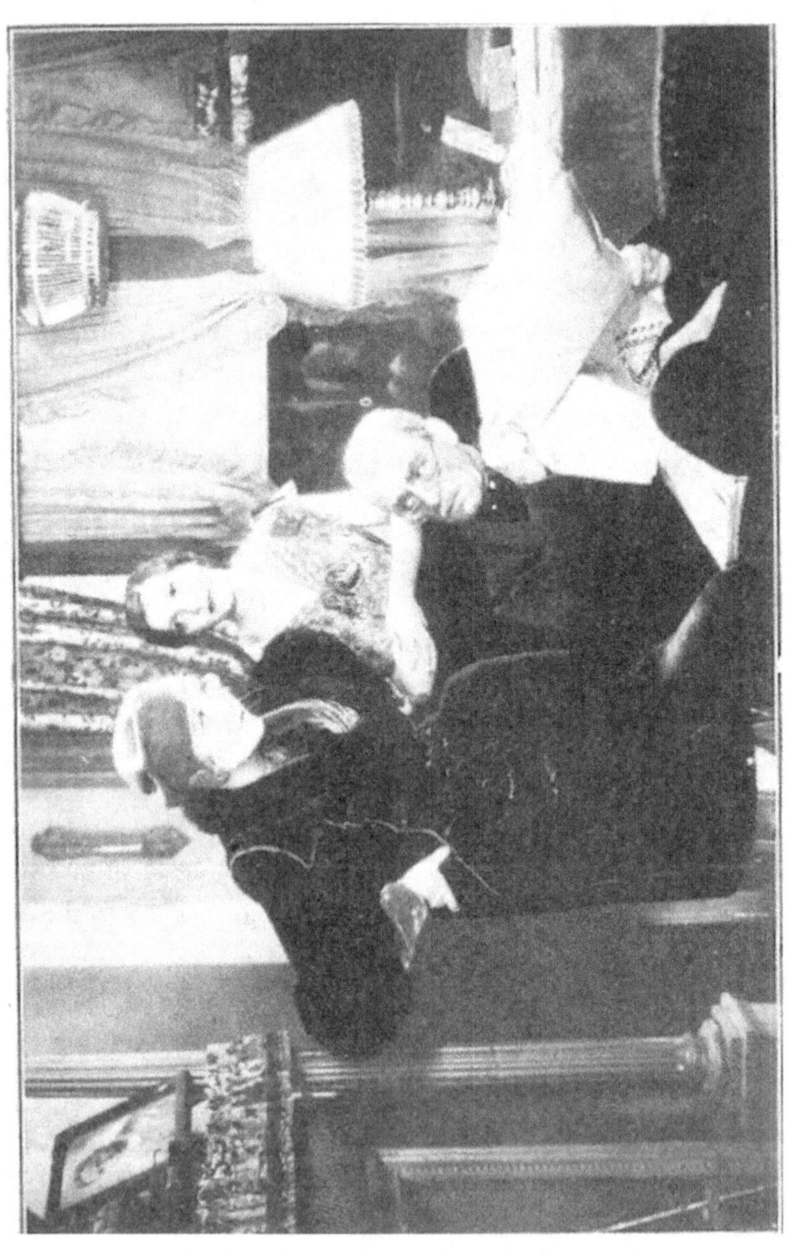

*"I think that your children are nicer than you."*

*"I am very good in the kitchen."*

on time, he will be happy!" Those were his last words"

Grumpy leaned a little more on the arm of his friend.

In just a few minutes, he had grown old again, and his sobs had grown quieter...

He murmured:

"What grief! What grief!"

But he didn't know what else to say.

"My old friend Grumpy, in this painful time, you can believe that all your friends are with you with all our hearts"

This was the phrase that Jeff had prepared and which he was uttering, as if out of the blue, at the conclusion of this painful meeting. But his emotions could not remove the banality of the phrase.

"It's the job" he added.

"It's the job" echoed Grumpy.

Then, after a pause:

"How am I going to tell Molly and Davey? To this young girl who loved him so much, to my grandson who cherished him! Ah! My god! My god! They will never see him again! It would have been better if it had been me!"

"Grumpy, you have been courageous all your life. You must continue to be so now...."

At that moment Tommy appeared.

"What's going on? What?"

"Your brother..."

"My brother?...And what?"

"He's been involved in an accident"

"Is he dead?"

The two men remained silent.

Then Tommy broke down in tears.

"You must be brave, my son" said Grumpy. "Have courage like me"

But a rage seized the younger man.

"Oh! You!...you!...that's all that comes out of your mouth...duty...courage...you mouth these words! Everything must yield to this....this abominable job that we do, that you do, it's like a priesthood....It's easy to say "Have courage"...Poor Jim!"

"That's enough Tommy! Calm down"

"No, it's not enough, I won't be calm....He died for a lousy job..I'll die for it...we'll all die for it...Idiots who are searching for our way here, because you have pushed us, because you have seen what we have not, that we should not do anything else...And you carry on...You have also given a locomotive to your grandson...to give him a taste for the job. Poor little Davey! You will also launch him onto the railways...if he listens to you....And see now....he is fatherless. And this poor fatherless boy, it's you who have done this..."

"Tommy! You are too cruel! You cannot say such things..."

"Yes...Yes...you are responsible for his death, since it is you who sent him into this danger"

"My god! My god!" wailed Grumpy suddenly, stunned by his sons pain and his reproaches.

"But at least tell me how he died"

And the sad messenger told him the whole story.

"Ah! Yes!" he sneered when the man was finished "I see it all now...Yes..."Tell my father that the train that was blocked will be on time!" This was his last concern...

Yes...Yes..the train must not be late...Be happy now father! The train left on time and you have one son less..."

His voice broke with renewed sobbing.

As if ashamed by his tears, he turned away, then without a word, ran away.

Grumpy remained there, frozen to the spot.

"How am I going to tell Molly this terrible news? How? How?"

"You will find the words you need Grumpy..Goodbye"

And with that Jeff left.

Around old Anderson there was nothing but emptiness.

Awkward at being consoled, he excluded his colleagues from his excruciating pain.

So, he took off his work clothes, got dressed and left.

As he disappeared, his head bowed, his step was heavy and unsteady.

He was going to be the messenger of death.

And his heart was bleeding.

# CHAPTER IX

Tommy Anderson had worshipped his brother.

His brother's tragic death was the most painful thing he could conceive of in his life.

His mood darkened.

He could not breath in this house, once so happy, where death had come.

And his job seemed harder and sadder.

He did his work with hatred.

He had to live, however, and not leave Molly and Davey alone with their grief.

But he did not feel he was up to this role.

Time had not erased the grudge that he held against his father. Their relationship was no longer as loving and trusting as it had once been.

He didn't feel that special closeness to Grumpy Anderson anymore. It seemed only that they were simply two links in the same chain.

It was a silent hostility between them which overruled filial respect.

*Would they cut Davey in two, as if they were Solomon?*

*"All's good" he said. "Let's eat!"*

What he needed himself was consolation and tenderness. But who would give him that?

Consumed by his hard work, returning home worn out, his job for the day finished, where could he look for distractions?

Zella?

Certainly, the name of the young girl, whose kiss still burned, returned often to his mind. She could perform miracles. But did she care?

He could not, in fact, completely convince himself that it was not just a beautiful dream. This fictional romance he seemed to be living in seemed like something impossible, imaginary. Was it not madness to chase after this mirage?

One evening, however, he could stand no more.

Never mind, after all!...He had the right to be entertained as well.

It was after dinner, sad like all the meals now in this bereaving house. He went to dress.

He no longer hid from his father the fact that he was going out.

"Where are you going?" asked Grumpy Anderson nevertheless.

"I don't know myself father. But" - and there was a ferocious irony in his words - "I will go there for the train to leave on time"

And he headed off in the direction of the Paralta Club.

He was in no rush to arrive, because this walk was like a pilgrimage. He remembered his first visit to Zella, curious and shy. His heart had beat so strongly, that evening, wondering what he would find.

It was an adventure and nothing more. And its strangeness only attracted him.

But it had taken such a delightful turn!

"Zella! Zella!" he muttered to himself in a modest plea.

He walked on, reflectively.

Was he really allowed to make this new visit? Was he just going to be a nuisance?

He decided not to go to Zella Maybelle's dressing room, where he had already chanced his arm.

He would simply be an ordinary customer who wanted to kill some time...He would rather wait for her to recognise him....She would have to call to him or come to see him, if his presence was agreeable.

It was discreet, appropriate.

He entered, and straight away, he felt uneasy and dizzy. The noisy cheerfulness of this establishment where everything was designed and executed for joy, was too much of a contrast to the pain he carried. The music, the laughter, the girls shrieking, made him ache. He was about to leave. He was afraid he was going to cry.

But he overcame this weakness.

The table where he had sat that first visit, was free just then. He recognized it straight away and settled himself there.

After a moment, it seemed to him that he had left his sadness at the cloakroom.

The performances followed, one after another, during which he hoped again to catch a glimpse of Zella.

A little mousey blonde girl, graceful and pale, came

up to him and smiled. He barely noticed her. "You don't have a wild, fun air about you"she said.

"But if.."

"You don't want me to keep you company? You'd like to dance later?"

"I never dance"

"Ah well! We will talk instead!"

But Tommy couldn't show any enthusiasm.

"You're waiting for someone, perhaps?" she asked him.

"You have guessed"

"Oh! Well in that case..."

And she left him to his solitude.

He looked around curiously. All the beautiful girls who didn't have to try to be pretty; these hilarious men who never seemed to have any problems whatsoever, appeared to him as different beings, incomprehensible.

He had a reason to be there, but they?

Zella Maybelle had still not appeared.

"I hope she's not ill" he thought to himself.

And this thought was painful to him.

He had already seen all the attractions. He was surprised that the hostess was not there.

"Gone?"

But yes, why not? She had perhaps fled with...yes, why not, with that man who spoke so roughly, who she seemed to be afraid of, and who he, Tommy, had so severely punished...was it possible?...She belonged to him, after all....

If he had had neighbors at his table, they would have seen him pale and blush alternatively.

This thought was odious to him.

But he could no longer get it out of his head.

Yes, that was it! Zella had scrammed, god knows where, the perfect love story! He had been forgotten, him, poor Tommy, locomotive driver!

And, from that moment on, with that rare inconsistency of lovers, his only thought was to trample his love.

The jealousy gnawed at him. It filled him with spite and bitterness.

Ah! Zella, she had gone!

Ah well! He would look for another. He had lost one, but found ten!...

The little blonde who had recently come to him, passed by again. He called to her.

"Ah! Sir changed his mind!"

"Yes. Come and sit down here. What's your name?"

"Lizzie"

She was a little hectic woman, stimulating, funny.

She talked passionately yet said nothing.

She chatted thoughtlessly. She exaggerated everything, her joy, her surprise, her laugh, her irritations.

"I like you alot Mr. Tommy"

She let herself be kissed with ease. She breathed with a sort of juvenile sensuality.

They danced in order to get to know each other better. She was light in his arms, like a feather, and he wrapped her completely in his embrace.

"Do you come here often" she asked him.

"No, rarely"

"Yet it seems I have seen you here before?"

"It's possible"

Their conversation lacked animation and variety.

They soon ran out of things to say to fill the silence between the jazz tunes or between the songs.

Yet she waited for him to whisper some tender words to her.

And he also wanted to be able to say something.

But he could not.

Something stronger than his will kept him from saying the words he had prepared, those words of love, always the same, both eloquent and banal.

It seemed like he could not break free, afraid of messing up.

Only Tommy's hands talked.

But when, after a kiss, she put her ear against his lips, Lizzie never heard "I love you".

Soon the rest of her colleagues came over to join them.

The time was getting on. A good number of diners had already left. There were now lots of empty tables and lots of pretty girls with nothing to do.

In this chirping company, brushed by ones arm, by the leg of another, embraced by a raven haired girl, caressing a redhead, Tommy started to lose his grip on reality. He was living the night of a mogul, without other concerns, other than to forget.

But suddenly he jumped. During a conversation he hadn't really been listening to, he had been startled to hear the name of Zella mentioned.

"Zella" he said. "Which Zella?"

"But Zella Maybelle, of course!"

"Ah! Well!"

"Oh my! But what is she to you?" remarked one of the girls. "Is she your sister?"

"Tell me what you said!"

"Why we said that she has gone!"

"With who?"

He had become livid.

"With who? But what's it got to do with you?"

"I asked you"

"She left alone, like she often does, on tour. Zella is a reliable woman you know"

He breathed heavily.

He felt as though a great weight had been lifted, that he had hope again.

Zella had left alone!

There was no reason to think that she had forgotten him. Why should she? Perhaps at this very moment she was thinking of him...

But then? What was he doing? In this company?

Abruptly he got up.

"You're leaving already?" they asked, astonished.

"Yes...yes..right away...Good evening"

And he almost bumped into them in his haste to leave.

"He is a little crazy, I think" said the little blonde.

He returned home much faster than he had left. He was furious with himself. He could have kicked himself.

The kisses that he had stolen from Zella remained with him, like a taste of ashes.

By what aberration had he wronged her? This heart

that he loved.

But there was no longer any doubt possible. He loved Zella Maybelle!

Love inconsiderate, mad love, vain desire..possibly. But since when was passion rational? Since when was sentiment reasonable?

Did he have a chance? No, not according to the accepted conventions.

But was that a reason not to try?

He was not simply a driver's assistant, he had become an engine driver and this was still not enough to dazzle Zella. But he was not able to do anything else. Was he destined to do this job by birth? Could he not also make a success of other things?

"She is not aware of anything, happily!" he thought to himself.

Because men do not like to remain too long in their head to head with their ignominy.

When he arrived home a single thought filled him, he needed to change his life. He had to conquer Zella. This he wanted above all.

What could he do? He knew nothing. But that wasn't important! Fortune, claimed the proverb, favoured the bold.

He was discovering all his boldness. It was not so foolish. He did not baulk at the task ahead. Why not success, he sulked?

The difficulty was to admit to his father that he wanted to change his life.

Certainly, since the death of Jim, and perhaps unjustly in his pains, he had been freed from parental ties.

but he had had to fight hard against a grip of twenty years and against the obedience of youth.

Could he find the opportunity before it was too late?

"I am master of my own destiny" he stated aloud.

And he gave a great blow to his chest.

....But as all were asleep in the little house, he entered quietly on tiptoes, so as not to wake anyone.

It was so late, and he had so little time left to sleep!....

# CHAPTER X

Grumpy and Tommy Anderson were transported to the hospital on two stretchers.

And the investigators set to work to find the causes of the accident. It had not been just an accident, but almost a disaster without precedent.

The train driven by Grumpy Anderson, with Tommy as his assistant, had sideswiped a freight train. The shock of the impact on the train buffers had derailed the wagons of the freight train. But by a miracle, the express train had not suffered. Only the locomotive was knocked over on the rails.

Given the speed the trains were travelling at when they collided and the circumstances of the accident, it could have been a lot worse.

However, there was not one death. Only two injuries: Anderson and his son.

How had the accident been caused? Who was responsible?

On examination, the signals seemed to have worked perfectly. The freight train, which had had a slight delay to its schedule, was equipped with the regulation lights. The signals had been ignored. The fault therefore had been committed by the engine driver.

However, they could not accuse Grumpy of recklessness. During all the years he had worked for the Company, when he had driven the fastest trains, never had his attention wavered and never had he made a mistake. Never had he been reproached by the company for anything.

He was a slave to his duty and scrupulously conscientious.

It was also well known that he was one of the most skilled locomotive drivers in the United States, one that was not afraid of any dangers, but who was cautious and calmly bold.

On the other hand, the night was very clear. No fog obscured the signals. It was impossible that he had not been able to see. The first witness to be heard was the conductor of the express train.

He explained before the Commission:

"We were rolling along at about 110 an hour, normal speed for this part of the track, when suddenly I was thrown among the baggage by a great shock.

"The train stopped suddenly and I rushed outside to see what had happened.

"Cries of terror were coming from all the cars. But the damage couldn't have been very great, since all the cars were still standing upright on their wheels and intact. I went up to the front of the train. The first car, where there was no one, was the only one to have suffered. But the engine was lying on its side.

"From pipes, burst in the shock of the collision, jets of steam were escaping and their hissing was drowned out by the calls of distress of the driver, Grumpy Anderson. Covered in blood, half buried under the coal which had rolled out of its tender, the driver tried to lift his assistant who, more seriously injured, was trapped between two iron bars and was close to the gaping furnace, at risk of being atrociously burned.

"With the help of the brakeman and some of the passengers who had run to the scene, we freed, firstly Grumpy Anderson who was the easiest to reach. We were then able to reach and rescue his son Tommy and were able to remove him from this perilous situation.

"It was an atrocious scene. The father, who we had tentatively laid down on the grass, wouldn't stop crying "I have killed my son! I have killed the only son I have left!..It's my fault!...It's my fault!..." And he begged us: "Leave me to die, but save him!"

"It took us a good quarter of an hour to pull Tommy out from where he was trapped. He had wounds to his head and was bleeding profusely. But he was still breathing and managed to say a few words: "We shot through the signals" he murmured. Alerting the nearby station for the transfer of the passengers, we carried the wounded.

"That's all I saw. For me there is no doubt: the signals were obscured - I can't explain how - and were not seen by the driver. He didn't have time to stop the train when he saw it was on a collision course with the freight train. But the fact we don't have any dead to mourn is certainly down to the unparalleled skill and great coolness of Grumpy Anderson who handled his locomotive with an absolute mastery, reducing to a minimum the terrible consequences of the collision".

This testimony, the confession of Grumpy Anderson: "It's my fault!", that of Tommy: "We shot through the signals", could hardly leave any doubt as to who was responsible for the accident.

Anyway, once the two wounded were able to be interviewed, these were the established facts.

"I could not, at that moment, keep watch on the way ahead" said Tommy, "because I was feeding coal into the furnace. It was when I suddenly turned round that I saw the error. My father hadn't discerned, no doubt, the color of the last signal. I shouted to him, but it was too late".

There were yet more investigations, discussions, experts and counter-experts. During several weeks they worked on the investigation. Because it was important that the Company could provide to the newspapers an explanation of the facts that would not put them in a bad light. Although there had been no casualties among the passengers, it was necessary, given the publicity surrounding the accident, that the public should feel reassured.

After sometime, they finally had reassuring news about the two injured. There would be no fatality. All danger had passed. They just needed a convalescence, more or less lengthy, depending on how they reacted to the treatment provided.

And it gave them chance to herald the news that the accident, bad as it had been, had resulted in no fatalities.

And everything was confined, according to the cliche, to damage to equipment which must be entered in the profit and loss account of the Company.

Old Grumpy Anderson, alone, accepted things less philosophically. It was not his own fate that he lamented, but that of his good old locomotive which he loved with a tenderness, almost sensual, which had never failed him, which had never refused his urgings, and which he had stupidly destroyed, in a moment of aberration.

"It's my fault! It's my fault!" he sobbed when the delirium overtook him.

# CHAPTER XI

The two wounded were placed in different rooms.

They were given the best, most dedicated care possible. Their injuries, on further examination, weren't as serious as originally feared. It was just a question of time until the healing took hold.

Tommy, young and strong, was the first on his feet. and leave the hospital.

Grumpy's recovery was slower. His old body was worn out. And his spirits weren't the best.

Some of his old friends came to see him, bringing news of the outside world. They brought a little of that air he loved to breath because he could smell on their clothes the wonderful smell of the coal, which another nose would not notice.

"Good morning, my old friend Jeff! It's a great pleasure to see you!"

"Well, you are looking better, you are on your feet now!"

"Yes...Yes...But I am bored and I know nothing

about Tommy. I've had no news. He has been kept somewhere else. Nothing is clear"

"Be reassured on this subject, I beg you"

"You have news?"

"Yes"

"Good news?"

"Excellent news"

"Ah! You bring me good news. You would not believe how much remorse I feel...I sometimes think if I have not been wrong to force my children to follow my tastes. I have lost one son, I almost succeeded in killing the other...I have spent many nights full of nightmares, in this bed....."

"Calm yourself, my old friend! Calm yourself!"

"But if Tommy is better, if Tommy is up and about, why hasn't he been to see me? To pay me a little visit?"

"Tommy is no longer in the hospital Anderson"

"Where is he?"

"He left"

"But then, what about me?...."

"Listen to me Anderson. I don't want to cause you pain, but it is necessary that you know certain things.... Remember, I was with you when, after the tragic death of Jim, Tommy reproached you with a misplaced anger and blamed you. He does not have the notion of duty that you have. He said to you: "You will kill us all". In this unhappy accident that has just happened to you, he has found a new reason to revolt. In his resentment, he has lost all sense of respect that a son should have for his father. He had, of course, news of you. But he never agreed to see you, you who he considers the cause of all his misfortunes. He left without saying anything...."

"But he has returned to the train depot?"

"No"

"But then, where has he gone?"

"Who knows?..."

"Ah! I am being well and truly punished!...." moaned Anderson, heaving a sigh. "Yet I never did what I am being blamed for"

"That's life!" said Jim, not knowing what else to say.

# CHAPTER XII

Grumpy Anderson also eventually left the hospital, but he left without joy. Something was missing from his heart, which he felt was irreplaceable.

As he left, a voice clearly rang in his ear.

"Hello, father Anderson!"

"You!"

"I was just coming to look for you. And here you are. Would you like some company? If I were a minute later I would have missed you"

"That is why we must always be on time!"

"Oh! I know papa Anderson, that is your pet subject!....But here you are looking quite well! It really doesn't look like you just spent several weeks in bed! Good men always come through!"

"Thank you miss"

"Ah! It's nice to see you smiling at me! Really, it is better than when I met you at your home"

It was Zella Maybelle who had called him.

"I had to come today" she continued , "because

tomorrow I leave on tour with my show. I wanted to be reassured on the fate of the grumpy engine driver who one day, despite himself, rendered me a lovely service!"

"Oh! Don't mention it!"

"But yes. Finally you see it like that. I am happy...."

She tenderly took his hand.

Grumpy Anderson had removed his cap, ready to say goodbye, when suddenly an idea popped into his head.

"Miss....tell me, in all sincerity and in confidence... did you go to see Tommy in the hospital?"

She blushed slightly, then:

"But naturally I went to see him!"

"Then, would you give me some news of him?"

"You must now that he has recovered"

"This I know....But since?"

"Since, I know nothing. One beautiful day, like today, I came here. But I had less luck that time. He had gone, without any fanfare"

"Without even saying goodbye..."

"Oh, you will see him again papa Anderson...."

"I hope so!.....But you can't tell me were I will meet him again?"

"I do not know. He didn't leave me his address"

"Ah! I am so unhappy!" concluded Anderson.

"There is no point dwelling on sad things, my good friend! You've come a long way, and life should feel beautiful to you!"

"Yes...yes...."

"Come on now, shake off this melancholy mood, and shake hands with me! Goodbye, papa Anderson"

"Goodbye Miss!"

*Both, carefully, placed her in her car.*

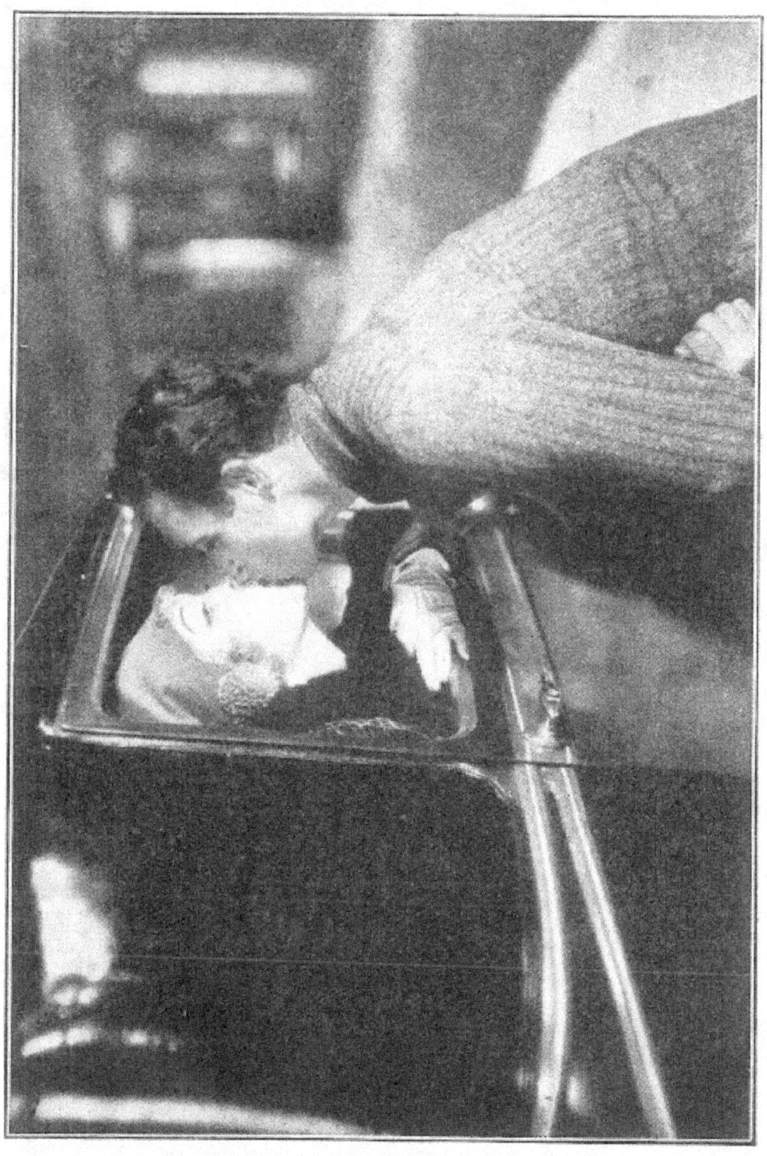

*Their hot lips, alive, vibrant, met.*

*You can tell my father that thanks to Jim the train left on time.*

*No one dead; Only two injured. Anderson and his son.*

He watched her for a moment as she left. And he regretted, because this poppet was the only consolation he had in his sorrow.

# CHAPTER XIII

Grumpy Anderson had been an excellent employee, for which he was held in high regard.

During his convalescence, the Company was very guarded, leaving aside the sanctions that would be taken against him, following the accident from which he had escaped.

But when he returned home, he found this letter pinned to his front door:

CHICAGO & NORTHWEST RAILWAY COMPANY

To Mr. Anderson

"Dear Sir,

The Commission of Enquiry met to examine the causes of the accident that occurred to the train that you were driving, and has concluded that it was your responsibility. You no longer meet the requirements required of a driver of express trains. And we are obliged to withdraw you from this work. But, in regard to your long service and also the splendid work record you have with us, we will keep you on our payroll, for a subsequent assignment

Yours faithfully

J. J. Brenman, Managing Director"

Twice, three times, twenty times, Grumpy Anderson reread this damned letter which spelled out his downfall.

So, from now on, he would be considered as a good for nothing!

He, who just yesterday, was rightly given the title of one of the best engine drivers of the North West Company, who was an example, who was asked to do what others were not able to do; thus he, whose whole perilous life was doomed by intransigent duty, was purely and simply scrapped, like an old machine!

He tottered.

His life was shattered! It was worse than the disaster which had injured his body.

It was his heart, now, which needed attention....

He clung to the wall so as not to fall.

# CHAPTER XIV

The next day, Grumpy Anderson returned to his workshop.

He was eager to be returning to familiar surroundings, to meet his old workmates again, to especially see the locomotives again.

He was greeted with genuine warmth. Everyone respected him for his admirable dedication and also for his mastery of the job. They gave him a warm welcome.

But their sympathy was not enough to calm the torment he suffered.

"What will become of me?" he asked the Depot Manager, in a voice half imploring, half full of hatred.

"But, there's always a home for you here Grumpy. You stay with us. There are other things you can do other than drive the great express trains. Sometimes things must change in life"

Anderson shook his head.

"It would be better if it never changed"

Old Grumpy was put to work in the repairs workshop.

There he had to supervise a team of fitters, boilermakers etc...

But, he himself, also threw himself into the job, happy for his hands to feel the sides of these steel monsters which, though cold, seemed to live.

He examined and touched them with a sort of romantic fervor.

Only, when he climbed onto the machines and took the place that had for so long been his, when he turned the handles, nothing happened. And he felt a surge of nostalgia. He was disappointed and helpless, like a child with a beautiful but broken toy.

He had to learn to take his pain with patience.

"When this engine is repaired, they will give it to me to try out" he thought to himself.

But when it left the workshop, it was another that took it and threw it back into the hectic and dangerous life on the rails.

He was somewhat ashamed of the lessening of his status. And, as much to deceive himself as to hide his decline from others, he told anyone who would listen:

"I am low now. But they promised me soon, an engine more beautiful than the one I used to drive, a modern engine, I will be its first master"

But he did not convince anyone.

However, she arrived one day, this famous engine. She arrived at the workshop for repairs and in a pitiful state. She required full repairs and a total overhaul.

It was engine 2.329. "Thunder".

He knew her well and recognized her immediately. He uttered a cry of joy on seeing her, like welcoming a parent after a long absence.

Here was 2.329!

It was still his locomotive, one he had driven through so many pitfalls and perils. It was with her that he had laughed at delays; it was partly thanks to her that he had always been rated as the model of an engine driver, an example to others. Through her obedience, through her valor as well, she had brought so much joy to old Grumpy.

And it was also with her that he had been injured, with her and with Tommy. This though brought him a new remorse.

He felt guilty about his son, about her, his engine, also.

She had rushed headlong, meeting all of Grumpy's commands and desires, with all her might, all her power. She went, blindly, knowing well the way ahead, without risks, while he was watching out for her. And his stupidity, he did not know how, had precipitated the disaster.

But he could remake her into something again!

He owed her that.

"Ah! If I know anything, it's this engine" he said to his workers. "I know her by heart. All the nuts, all the bolts. There is not an inch of her that I have not caressed, polished. I know her like I know my child. I know how she runs, I know what she thinks, she is in my heart"

For the moment, his heart was dead. He had to rebuild her.

Never had he worked with so much heart on a machine. Nor with such haste either.

Grumpy Anderson was anxious to see the wheels turn again, to hear the roar of one of those rages of insensible things.

Unhappily, although she looked good, in spite of all his care, she would never be what she once was.

She could be patched up; she would run again, but she would no longer have that ardor, that courage, that nerve that he had known.

She would end up at the head of a goods train, one of the convoys which go slowly, stopping at every station, breathless, asthmatic, having to give way to the proud, fast express trains.

She had grown old, like her master.

Ah well! Never mind. Grumpy loved her enough to accept this humiliation. We will pull the goods wagons! We will take one small step at a time!

Provided they went together!

Even if it were in the sidings, they would, Grumpy and her, be able to execute small maneuvers, form trains, divert the cars, small simple tasks that are entrusted to veterans.

Grumpy Anderson had the job in his blood.

The day when they would finally permanently remove his right to work, would be the day he would die.

# CHAPTER XV

Extremely violent storms battered the South. During those days, the rain fell with an intensity unheard of. The ground, full of water, was unable to absorb it all, and the rivers, full in their beds, had soon broken their banks and overflowed.

Everyone had believed, at first, that the flooding was localized, that the rising water would quickly find its high mark and recede without the local population having suffered.

But one night of torrential downpour was enough to precipitate events and cause a disaster.

A small stream had grown suddenly into a raging torrent, rushing down the valley like a tidal wave.

In the blink of an eye, the level of the water rose dramatically.

The dams, which had previously held, were broken under the impact of trees caught up in the floodwaters and by the debris of bridges swept away by the current.

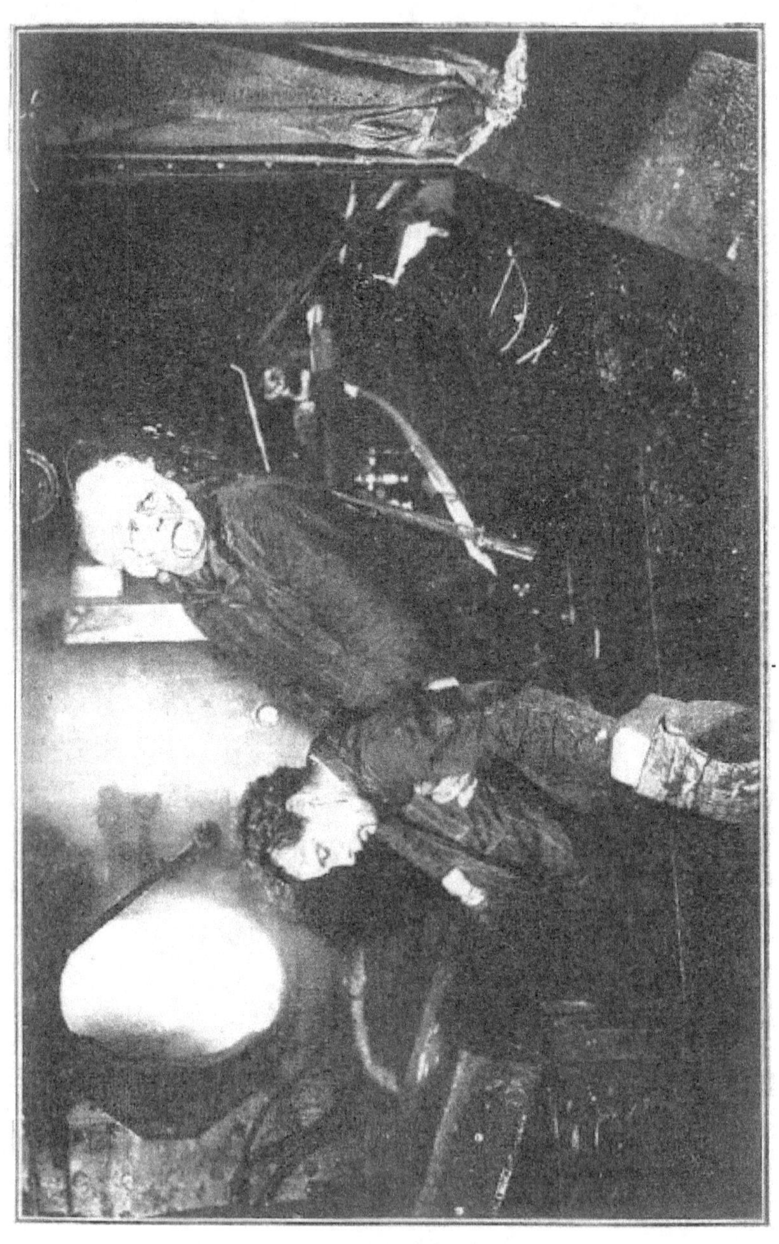

*The engineer struggled to free his driver.*

*Candid:Chaney greats the real life railroad expert, a Mr. Pruner.*

And it was frightening in its devastation.

The waters first engulfed the homes in the low laying areas, then spread, little by little, and those who had believed themselves safe became alarmed.

On all sides came requests for help. But those calling for help, who still had telephones or any means of information, were the lucky ones.

During the night the tragedy became clear, by the glow of lightning, and somehow relief was organized. But most efforts proved powerless.

A boat launched into the current and was almost lost. Failure was not due to lack of courage or the heroism of the rescuers.

Those pitiful scenes were painful to behold! There was, on the roof of a house already submerged, a woman holding her child at arms length, in the hope that someone would save it; and others struggling, exhausted, dead tired in the slimy waters...

Young people, who had climbed to the top of a tree, their feet already in the swirling waves, suddenly let go and fell, seized by the water and carried away, unable to save themselves.

Old people were laughing and dancing on roves, suddenly becoming crazy.

There were only cries of distress to be heard, in the uproar of the wind and the crash of thunder.

Any serious, organized rescue became impossible. Chance alone guided the rescuers.

When the day dawned, the storm finally calmed. But the brilliant sun rose on a countryside absolutely desolated.

Nothing had been spared.

The river had extended, in some places, to several miles in width. The waves rolled furniture, cradles and beds, and corpses. Eddies formed on what had been village squares. Chimneys of houses floated, dismantled, grim, as if a bombing had caused their ruin.

The first statistics, hastily established, gave an enormous number of victims. The damage amounted, for certain, to millions of dollars.

Emotion was intense throughout the whole country. In over a century no such cataclysm had ever been seen.

Imaginations were knocked. And on all sides help was offered.

But good intentions were useless! It wasn't humanly possible to attempt anything until the roaring water had subsided, as an impassable barrier stretched between the ravaged region and the rest of the country.

Aircrafts rushed, carrying food that they threw onto the campsites where refugees and victims of the disaster huddled together.

But this supply was precarious. And the means employed did not match up to the scale of the disaster.

Whatever his ingenuity and his courage, man found himself disarmed in such circumstances!

In its anger, nature was much stronger.

This time, she was ruthless.

# CHAPTER XVI

"So, Tommy, your resolution is final?"

"Yes, Mac, I will never again do the job I was doing. I value my skin too much. It was quite a serious warning I had, I believe."

"One dies only once"

"Of course. But I did not want to die then. I don't want to spend my days and nights, like a devil in his hell, skin burning, eyes burning, lungs burning"

"But what are you going to do then?"

"I don't know....I will have to have a think"

If Grumpy had been looking forward to resuming his life after his release from the hospital that had temporarily interrupted it,his son had not shown the same kind of enthusiasm.

He had benefitted from the convalescence which he had been granted and cared only to steer his life in a different direction.

At the hospital, as soon as he could move, his first thought had been to write to Zella Maybelle.

He had sent a very simple letter, very short, very to the point.

He said:

"You certainly will not come, Miss Zella, to the hospital to see the little driver who suffers. I would only like to receive a word from you, saying that you think a little of me. My wounds would heal more quickly to know this - TOMMY"

And Zella came. She could not approach him as the rules forbade it. But she brought her news, and brought him some sweets, and a few words that made him feel better.

Better, and worse at the same time.

Because he dreamed of fresh air, of space, of the joy of being outside; because he dreamed of love....and that love was Zella....and Zella was not made for a driver of the North West Railway Company.

He left the hospital without seeing her again.

He did not even think of giving her his news, once he was free.

He was near to a nervous breakdown, totally discouraged, without anyone to console him.

After what had happened, after what had been said, he could not return to his father. He would have to wait until his rancor had cleared.

He tried, as he had done before, to offset his boredom by looking for the easy pleasure of the nightlife. But each time, he returned a little more sickened and disgusted with himself.

He thought of Zella obsessively, and she was the one to which he dared not go.

How would he get out of this? Leave the rut he had gotten into?

"Say, Tommy" said Mac "You saw what happened in the South?"

"The floods?"

"Yes"

"It was terrible!"

"But you did not see the appeal launched by the Company?"

"No, since I didn't return to work"

"Well, here, look! The Red Cross is organizing trains to help. And as it is quite dangerous to go there, where the water has washed away the roads, and perhaps rendered unusable those that people believe to still be in good condition, the Company did not want to force the hand of its employees. They are asking for volunteers"

"They found all they need?"

"I'm not sure because they need a great number"

"What! They probably haven't then!"

"You know...there is less generosity than we think"

"You are naturally going, Mac?"

"I must...I am young...and single..."

"You are right. Goodbye Mac"

"Goodbye Tommy'

# CHAPTER XVII

"What, Tommy! You are here! Your convalescence is finished?"

"I still have a few days..."

"But we thought you weren't coming back to the job?"

"We must do what it takes"

"Ah! You're back like before! And I bet you come as a volunteer? For the Red Cross trains?"

"That's not difficult to guess..."

Tommy had many friends among his workmates. And they all rejoiced to see him back among them. Moreover, they were all volunteers. And this surge of generosity, this youthful need for dedication inspired a healthy reaction in the souls of the young men. They were also caught up in the atmosphere of excitement.

"But that's not all!" he said "I did not come here to see trains pass like a gate keeper. When do we leave?"

"When there are some engines available"

"Then, I put my name down for the first"

"By what right?"

"By the right of one returning who wants to take revenge?"

"Well, then we leave it to you. We will allow him the first, will we not?"

"Yes....yes...."

"Well, Tommy, a supervisor has just come, so you will not have long to wait. He just called to say that an engine was ready. You can go to the driver"

"Let's go. Where is she?"

"On the turntable. It's there...wait while I look it up...it's engine 2.329"

The young man jumped.

"2.329? The bitch!"

"You know it then?"

"You might say that!...Oh, I know her well! We had some damage together..."

"Goodbye Tommy, good luck"

"Goodbye my friends!"

He went across to the depot. He could not help but smile bitterly. Destiny was strong! And it had ironic ways to manifest its power. Chance would not send him an engine he did not know! It was enough, thank God! But no! It was that it was precisely as it had been during his first revolts! When he had sworn he would no longer be the driver!....

But it was not a step back. Can we understand the feelings that were stirred up?

He entered the deserted depot, and he didn't have

*He himself, put his shoulder to the wheel.*

*It was still his locomotive, that he had often driven*

*"Tommy, they just telephoned to say an engine was ready"*

to search too long. Engine 2.329 was there, ready to go out, just waiting to be animated by a new Prometheus.

He looked with disgust at first, then he approached the engine. Here and there shone the bright steel and gilded copper new parts. They were like so many scars that she bore.

His bitterness dissolved into a kind of pity. She had also suffered, at the same time as him, in the same accident.

And here he was, perfectly willing to try a new adventure.

It was his destiny, and hers too.

He climbed aboard. He recognized and found his place, where he had so often watched, with eyes fixed, thoughts concentrated....also where one day during an icy storm, Zella Maybelle had insinuated her delicate little body....

He turned several times, like a tenant who enters his apartment after a long journey and seeks the welcome of familiar objects.

Then, rolling up his sleeves, he seized his hammer and began to break into small pieces the coal that he threw onto the glowing wood, which would give life to engine 2.329.

# CHAPTER XVIII

"As long as they don't give me an assistant who drives me nuts!" said a voice suddenly from the engine.

Tommy jumped, he recognized the voice of Grumpy Anderson.

This got better and better.

Without turning his head, he shouted back in the same tone:

"As long as they don't give me a driver who is a sham!"

He straightened up when he heart the footsteps of Grumpy Anderson on the deck of the locomotive.

"What! Tommy?"

"As you see!"

They looked fixedly at each other in a moment of silence, trying to penetrate each others souls.

Then, at the same time, they fell into each others arms.

"My son!..."

"My father!..."

"We will move forward as soon as the engine is heated up, OK?" said Grumpy after a moment.

"Whenever you want!"

It was a long convoy of goods wagons, full of food and clothing, which was destined for the stricken region, and it was the first one that had been able to run, because of the hazards in that direction. The only ones aboard were the two Andersons and a conductor. The wagons were silent and locked.

They moved off.

Ah! The 2.329 was not what she had been. She no longer bounded forward like she was ready to leave the rails, to break the rigid itinerary on this iron road.

She went quietly, panting, spitting steam with a sound like a sick cough. But she made every effort, quietly and the long line of cars rolled steadily behind her at an equal pace.

To be in control of her anew, Grumpy Anderson felt a sort of intoxication. Through his worry, it made him feel like a beginner. It made him, it seemed, young again.

The first part of the journey was easy and without incident.

The Red Cross train made its merry way, neither more nor less than any other goods train. But soon they arrived at the extreme limit, where traffic was stopped by the flooding.

And it was then that began the hard work.

They were now on an adventure and heading towards probable dangers.

They drove on a track that the water had barely just receeded from and which was not yet completely safe.

They moved cautiously knowing a landslide or derailment would spell disaster.

"We are again in a funny business!" said Tommy.

"We can come through it" proclaimed the optimistic father.

"I don't doubt it! Otherwise I would not be here! But it's still strange work!"

They were still just crossing the previously flooded area.

It was a very dangerous journey. One in which the water still completely covered the track.

Engine 2.329 moved forward. She produced huge sprays of water left and right as she went.

They travelled slowly, in the dirty flood waters which spread for miles across the countryside.

Suddenly, to be isolated in this muddy sea, they felt a shiver pass down their spines.

They did not see anything in front of them, other than the water, the slimy water. They had the impression that they were floating for a short time, on a sea ready to swallow them.

"Maintain the pressure" said Grumpy.

"Of course, father! But the tide will soon drown the boiler"

"I am sure that we will soon pass the flood waters"

"Me too, I hope so..."

They had seen many other journeys together, the Andersons, before this unexpected voyage. But they had never felt such distress.

They had the heart to fight against any enemy who showed themselves, but not against an invisible enemy....

And they did not see anything......

"Goddamn" said Grumpy, shaking his fist.

"You are right father, all is not lost, we must try our luck"

For hours they rolled along, into the unknown, piercing the waves moving treacherously through an immense pool. They had gone too far to be able to retreat. And a retreat, like their advance, could be a death sentence.

"Load on more coal" ordered Grumpy.

And Tommy replied with a smile....

"Go! Go! You can charge ahead...the way is clear... like it has always been..."

# CHAPTER XIX

The victims of the flood waited with impatience for the promised train bringing help, but still they didn't see it coming! Among them were many sick, in need of help, children missing their milk. Families lived in tents without comfort.

The young, obviously, devoted themselves to helping to the best of their ability; the women improvised as nurses and carers; it was the broadest and most touching camaraderie.

But this was not enough, when everything was gone. All eyes were tensely watching the horizon. They searched for the plume of smoke from the locomotive which was coming, a cherished vision which was, alas, still absent!

It was a beautiful morning, and the news had spread. They had learned through the wireless that a train was on the way, pushing its way incessantly through the flood waters towards them, barring an accident.

Ecstatic, everything validated building the makeshift camp on a hill down to the station, or at least what remained of it. The water had almost receeded and the steel rails shone in the pale sunlight. But large pools of water still extended across the land, here and there. Only the platforms fully emerged from the water.

"They are here! They are here!"

The cries of joy resounded throughout the entire camp. There, in a splash of glory, appeared the locomotive. It was getting slowly bigger as it made its way cautiously...soon it would be there...

Drunk with joy, the people embraced and kissed each other, crying, laughing. Deliverance was here....

Hope was reborn and the zest for life returned... they were saved!...

The train entered the station...the breaks squealed. The locomotive expired a last few puffs of steam, as if, exhausted by its journey, it was ready to faint after a final effort.

And really, this dangerous journey, without the possibility of stopping, had been for Grumpy and Tommy, a slow torture. They had rolled along for hours and hours, without allowing one second of failure, of inattention, of rest, in continuous apprehension of disaster.

Finally, they were here.

And the happiness they brought was their reward, a sweet reward like no other.

To stretch his legs, having come to a halt, Tommy Anderson jumped down onto the ground. The soldiers who were there rushed to him, and cheered with an excitement, which he couldn't understand.

They were, Grumpy and he, like two new Messiahs.

They defended themselves with modesty. What had they done other than their duty? This recognition even embarrassed them. It was out of all proportion.....

And suddenly there was a shout from the crowd:

"Tommy! Tommy!"

"Someone here knows you?"

He looked around, searchingly. But he had hardly turned his head, when the voice repeated in his ear:

"Oh! Tommy! I was sure we would be saved by you"

"Zella! You are here!"

"Yes, it's me, here. I was surprised like everyone else by the disaster, and, as you see, I am transformed for the moment into a nurse, trying to put a little joy into hearts, which is much needed..."

"Zella, how happy I am!"

"But it is your father who is with you...let me also go and thank him"

And she climbed up onto the engine.

The misery he saw before him, which he had come to alleviate, had moved old Grumpy, and he tried hard not to cry.

He forcefully pressed the hand that Zella offered.

"Ah well, papa Anderson, you did not chase me away today...Ah! You are indeed a good man..."

"I did my job. Let's get down"

Grumpy, in his turn received an ovation which added to his confusion.

By what miracle Zella Maybelle, the dancing star, the wild child who had triumphed in all the establishments of pleasure, the smiling and joyful woman; by what miracle was she in this place of desolation?

This really pretty girl, deserving of her reputation as a serious girl, who Tommy had gone to see on an evening much like this, when he wanted to forget at the Paralta Club in Chicago.

A child of show business, born to a mother who was a dancer and a father who was a magician, a perfect and united household. Zella had been accustomed from an early age to work and a good, honest life.

Growing up in the environment of music halls, in constant day to day touch with the artists, she enjoyed all the small illusions of their work. How many dramas had the big eyes of the child contemplated. How unhappily had she cried as she witnessed death and despair and misery, then full of success they had abandoned the stage.

Zella hadn't understood until later, a lot later, but her mind was strongly affected. She had seen the drama continue, for the same reasons still existed, bringing the same sufferings, the same despairs.

As a star, every night was a triumph, constantly surrounded by a group of suitors, reigning over them until the richest and boldest had conquered her heart, she accepted the enthusiasm of the public.

Indeed, how could she resist the call of wealth, a love that seemed to be sincere, she was like a rabbit caught in the headlights, a lark falling under the lead of hunters, the girl was doomed.

Intoxicated by promises, by the first days of happiness, she abandoned all. Firstly the occupation that had led to success, then the company she disdained, the directors and booking agents that she mocked; her wealth would not last forever.

Then, one beautiful day, while she was lost in love, her man spotted a new victim and he suddenly disappeared leaving her a cheque, and the horror of the situation made the unfortunate girl incapable of any reaction.

Not even knowing the figure, the cheque was spent without foresight. Then she had to look for work, still believing herself a star. Alas! She quickly became disillusioned, she turned to the directors and booking agents that she had laughed at and mocked, and the poor fool was still happy and grateful to get a little bit of work in the chorus line so as not to die of hunger.

Next to these daily dramas, Zella had the example of her parents, still happily together. Certainly, her mother had never had a very prominent position, marriage sometimes prevents growth; those who create success always hope for a possible future and when they see it's unfeasible they let it drop.

But their household had always been divinely happy, never neglecting their commitments. Where the magician was engaged, his wife always found a job, and their love life continued.

Very efficiently, heedless of the carefree life, they jealously put money aside and, now that their daughter had taken a job in her turn, they were retiring to a little house in the country, cultivating a little garden, keeping chickens, their sole distraction being the long letters from Zella.

Warmed by what she had seen and deeply psychologically affected, the young dancer had said something: as men sighed over her, she was certain of their interest, so had to give hope to each one.

Brave as she could be, with a sense of organization, she created a full dance troupe, dressed by her, performing her tableaux and her compositions, and as she was a vivacious girl, full of mirth and friendly with everyone, the booking agents and directors were always demanding her.

She had one important principle: do not stay for a long time in the same city, not only because the public becomes weary, despite the diversity of dances, but also because she was less likely to be harassed by the old drunkards bent on a conquest.

Earning a good living, Zella Maybelle was already saving her money, following the example of her parents; she was not yet thinking of retiring, but she was a woman of independent means.

She in no way sought wealth, but true love, a serious love, she looked for that with her heart and soul.

Chance commitments had led Zella and her troupe to this prosperous and cheerful land before the horrible cataclysm.

There were not, in this part of the country, the same type of pleasure establishments as in Chicago. Night clubs were unknown here, the people worked all day long and didn't want to sacrifice their hours of rest.

But, on the other hand, there was a very popular music hall, very busy and always looking for exciting new attractions that the booking agents endeavoured to provide.

Zella Maybelle's troupe did not lie about the reputation that preceded them. The day of their debut the room was packed, and the show was a brilliant success.

There was so much grace, so much charm, the acknowledgement that here was a true artist, that the applause was immediate.

It redoubled at the appearance of the star and since the first day the triumph only increased, attracting all the country to the music hall.

Since the beginning of the floods, the troupe of girls had been noted for their charity. Each evening they gave an extra performance for the victims of the floods, organized raffles, collections, and Zella was the organiser of this kindness and her smile opened the tightest wallets.

Better, in the ballroom of the music hall, unoccupied since the first misfortunes, she had organized a play room for the children of affected families and, in the mornings, having taken virtually no rest, she was near to the little ones, communicating the same eagerness as her comrades.

Transformed into mothers of families, the girls, images of gaiety and carefree, lavished their care on all the children, while others prepared the meals, did the laundry, mending clothes, others were asking door to door for provisions for all those hungry mouths.

Several young girls from the town had joined with the dancers, delighted to obey Zella, whose sympathy was contagious.

The manager of the music hall had the idea to close his establishment, but the pretty girl was able to dissuade him, saying that the night's show was a welcome diversion and it was a way to put to use all the overflowing joy and energy.

It was then that the disaster abruptly hit them, at the

time when very many spectators were out at the performance. These circumstances almost certainly avoided a greater disaster, preventing people from being surprised in their sleep.

Everyone did their duty, wonders of bravery and courage were achieved.

Zella never lost her head, having learned that the dams had broken, she immediately considered the worst and without waiting until it was too late, organized the evacuation of the children....

Dressed in a jiffy, the kids were directed to a small fort set high on top of a hill overlooking the town, where they would have nothing to fear. She was again lavishing her care on the injured who had been brought from all sides.

When the daylight finally came, a horrible picture appeared in all its horror. This place that was full of laughter several days before was now nothing but ruins, and what had happened here had happened in many places and from all sides victims were added to the grand total.

Nevertheless, the still destructive waters seemed to be tiring of its carnage and the victims , helpless for so long, tried to organise themselves and dress their wounds.

Zella Maybelle was an intelligent and sensible girl; she didn't do anything to bring her to the forefront, to give advice to those who were more qualified than her to deal with the misery.

She remained in place and leaving the affected children to the care of a number of women from the town, she devoted herself entirely to the injured, thus swelling the ranks of the volunteer nurses.

All women with heart are, indeed, born nurses and Zella was no exception. She was immediately the angel of this place of suffering, her adorable smile, her sweet face, her golden hair, seemed like a ray of sunshine in the middle of all the desolation.

No one could accuse the towns for a lack of foresight, when they could not for a moment have anticipated such a disaster would befall them. The town where the troupe of girls was, was well stocked, but in the face of such deprivation, help was needed right away.

It was important not to let discouragement overtake the unfortunates and the cheerfulness of Zella and her companions helped enable this. Their voices could often be heard singing an old lament to numb the pain of the unfortunate people.

But could all these attempts bring some comfort to the grim reality?

Despite the wonders of energy and selflessness it was necessary for people to acknowledge the horrible situation, since the promised and expected relief had not arrived.

When the wireless had announced that the rescue train was forcing its way through the flood waters and that it had come from the North West Company, Zella felt in her heart a violent jolt, she thought immediately of Tommy and his father.

The unfortunate survivors still doubted that help was possible and some were afraid, cursing fate, sure that the train was doomed to be lost for certain, and swallowed by the treacherous water along with the brave men who had dared such a journey.

The young girl had told them of the courage of engineers and drivers, she had spoken with enthusiasm, that these men were capable of overcoming all dangers, she had seen them in the snow, in freezing temperatures, achieve the goal that was assigned to them. Certainly they would be triumphant and thanks to them, their suffering and misfortune would be eased.

And the idea came to her that perhaps Tommy was onboard this locomotive, driving the relief train. An idea that she quickly discarded, as the young man had declared that he wanted to give up his job.

That was the tale that the rescuers were told, and Grumpy Anderson smiled tenderly, watching the pretty girl.

Zella Maybelle joined Tommy.

"Tommy, we met on a stormy day, and we found each other again after another storm. Thunder has played a role in our lives"

He looked eagerly, holding his shoulder. His eyes peered into the depths of her soul. And to see her smile, so close to his lips, he was dazzled,,,,

"I thought that you didn't want to drive the train any more Tommy' she said.

"Indeed, but this time was exceptional. They needed volunteers, didn't they? I believe, however, that this is my last journey..."

"It must be your last journey, Tommy"

"Why do you decide this?"

She moved closer to him.

"Because, if you wish, nothing will separate us"

"What!? You!...You!...."

He jumped with joy, wavered, almost fell.

But she was in his arms. And in front of the unfeeling 2.329, in front of Grumpy, in front of everyone, strong in their love, proud of their happiness, they joined their lips in a total offering of their youth.

THE END

*"Here they are! Here they are!*

*Thunder*
*Lobby Cards*

LON
CHANEY
IN
A
Metro-
Goldwyn-
Mayer
PICTURE
THUNDER

LON
CHANEY
IN
A
Metro-
Goldwyn-
Mayer
PICTURE
THUNDER

LON
CHANEY
IN
A
Metro-
Goldwyn-
Mayer
PICTURE
THUNDER

Next "Lost Film Series" volume. The lost Science Fiction film.

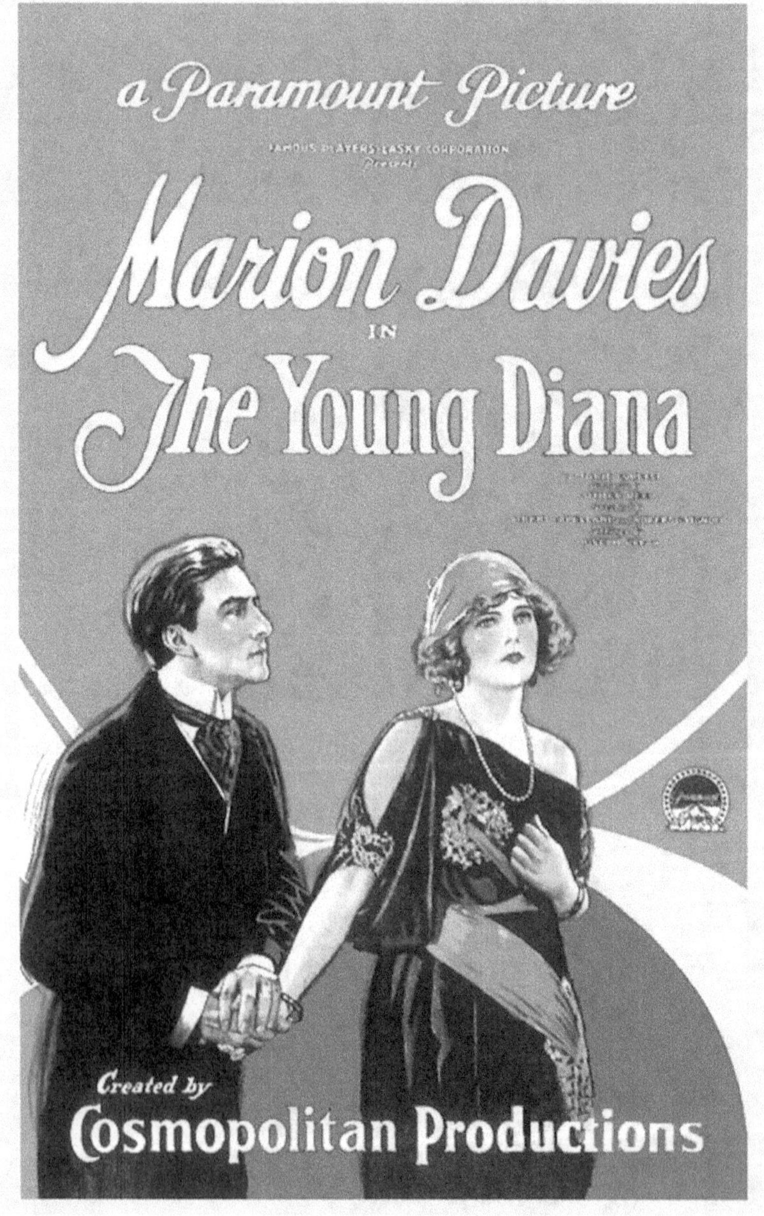

www.ingramcontent.com/pod-product-compliance
Lightning Source LLC
Chambersburg PA
CBHW060623310726
48982CB00003B/652

* 9 7 8 1 5 9 3 9 3 4 2 4 8 *